Mr Mullett
Owns a Cloud

Mr Mullett
Owns a Cloud

By Angela Locke
With illustrations by David Boyd

CUMBRIA *Life* BOOKS

First published in Great Britain in 1982 by Chatto & Windus
This new edition is published by Cumbria Life Books 2006
© Angela Locke 2006
Angela Locke asserts the moral right to be
identified as the author of this work.

Illustrations © David Boyd 2006

ISBN: 0952 00005742 92

Edited by Keith Richardson. Designed by Jonathan Law.
Printed by Thomson Litho, Glasgow
Cumbria Life Books, 51 Bank Street, Carlisle CA3 8HJ
is part of CN Group Limited
www.cumbrialife.co.uk

To my own grown-up children, Tessa, Emma and Harriet,
to my grandchildren, Amy, Joe, Sam, Ben, Kirsten and Niall
. . . and to all the grown-ups who have not yet forgotten that
there is still a little magic left in the world.

"Men have forgotten this truth," said the fox.
"But you must not forget it. You become responsible,
forever, for what you have tamed."
Antoine de Saint-Exupery: The Little Prince
in the translation by Katherine Woods.

Contents

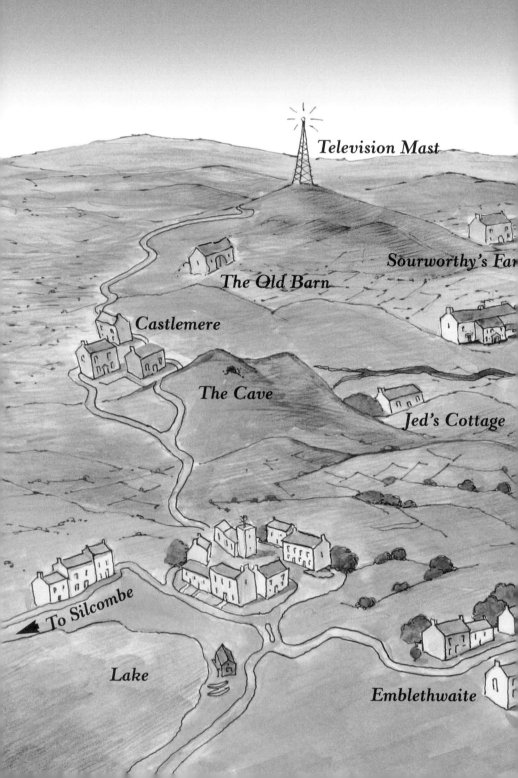

Television Mast

Sourworthy's Far

The Old Barn

Castlemere

The Cave

Jed's Cottage

To Silcombe

Lake

Emblethwaite

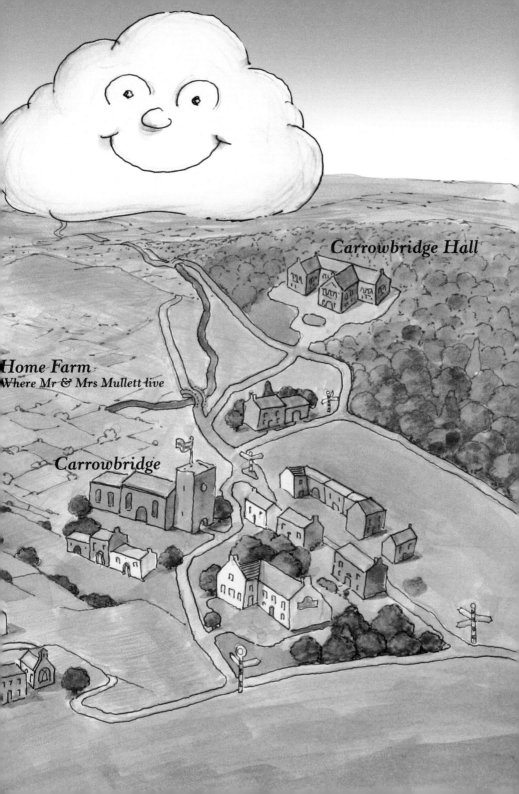

Carrowbridge Hall

Home Farm
Where Mr & Mrs Mullett live

Carrowbridge

ABOUT THE AUTHOR

Angela Locke MA

Angela Locke has had four fiction books published,
which have been translated across the world,
and three poetry collections. She has worked widely in
radio and television and leads international Creative
Writing retreats across the UK. Angela holds an MA in
Creative Writing from the University of Northumbria.
She lives in Cumbria where she is a columnist for
Cumbria Life magazine, and where she teaches Creative
Writing. Her new novel *Dreams of the Blue Poppy,*
which is set in Cumbria and the Himalayas, will be
published by Robert Hale in 2007. More detail on
Angela's work and books can be found on her website at
www.angelalocke.co.uk

How Napoleon found me

I am looking back at one of my early columns for Cumbria Life magazine in October 2001. I was writing about the day I climbed Carrock Fell for the first time in the late 70's, with the dear old Sherpa, otherwise known as Colin my husband, he of long patience and legendary load-carrying capacity.

Little did I know at the time this would be the day when the idea for my very first book would almost literally drop out of the sky.

The Sherpa used to commute to the City every day in his pinstripe, we hadn't long been married and our trips to Cumbria to stay with my sister in Welton were precious oases of peace and tranquillity in a busy and stressful life. It would be years before we could break the bonds and arrive to live in our beloved Cumbria full-time, with three kids in tow.

I had been script writing stories for the BBC Children's programmes, in those halcyon days when Little Ted and Jemima and the Square Window were the ultimate toddler chic. It was great fun. I used to attend rehearsals at BBC Television Centre and have lunch with the presenters and share the lift with John Craven and his ilk.

One day, I used to think, I'll write a book when I have the time. That day on Carrock Fell everything changed. I was climbing Carrock for the first time, into an enchantment, unaware that this

was the beginning of something new for me, something I would grow to love. Then came that life-changing moment, as we approached the summit, when Mr Mullett's cloud arrived in my mind. The Sherpa was almost out of sight when suddenly I was enveloped in an impenetrable fog. I could see a few feet in front of me, where the featureless path stretched upwards, but other than that I was surrounded by a grey blanket. The lark I had been listening to, as I struggled up the path, had been cut off in mid-trill. All sound had gone. I was panic-stricken. It was very cold and wet, my hair immediately beaded with moisture . . . then, as suddenly as it had arrived, the Celestial Scene-Changer whisked away the grey curtain of cloud and I was standing in blazing sunshine under a blue sky, the lark singing fit to bust. I almost heard a celestial giggle come from somewhere . . .

As we stood on the summit, I felt literally on top of the world. Sir Chris on top of Everest could not have been more ecstatic. Then the Celestial Scene-Changer did it again. One minute, a panoramic vista of fells as far as the eye could see, sun sparkling, blue sky, larks (as above) a raven looping the loop, then . . . whack! Nothing. Dark, grey, nothingness; a rainy Sunday afternoon with 'Sing Something Simple' on the radio, cold tapioca, school lunches (old style) and having to do your maths homework before Monday . . . I stood clutching the summit cairn, shivering in the cruel wind, consoling myself with the last crumb of Mars Bar, when whoosh! it happened again, with a chuckle. Brilliant rock colours. Mountain vistas.

Later that day, back at Welton, I was staring out of the window, trying to see where we had been on Carrock. But the entire fell had

disappeared. Where before there had always been a spectacular view out of the sitting room window, now there was nothing. The sky was blank. Low cloud had come down and wiped Carrock out. I remembered my experience with the cheeky cloud on the top. I caught myself wondering what it must be like to live on the side of a mountain. When the cloud comes down, I remember thinking, and you open the kitchen door, it must all come inside. All that cloud! It must be part of your world!

And then the title *Mr Mullett Owns a Cloud* just popped into my head. In that moment, Napoleon, the delinquent cloud, was born and took on a life of his own. I have no idea where it all came from. Mr Mullett's name was a mystery too. I didn't even know any Mulletts, but years later when the original book reached New Zealand, I had a letter from an old sheep farmer called Mullett whose family had come from Whitehaven. Had I based the old fell farmer of my book on any of his family? I still treasure the letter and wish I could have said 'Yes!'

The book took several years to write, and included many research visits to Cumbria to stay with my long-suffering sister Stephanie, poring over copies of *The Cumberland News* and listening to a Cumbrian dialect tape so many times, day and night, that the Sherpa threatened to throw it out of the window. Eventually, I got a letter from the Editor at Chatto & Windus saying they loved the book and in due course that magic day arrived in October 1982 when the book became a published reality.

The national launch began in Cumbria and extended across the country via radio and television. I had written the book to appeal to

children as well as adults, and it proved very popular with both. It has a 'magic' element, but the underlying themes are very down to earth and real.

The first signing was at The Bluebell bookshop in Penrith, then a tiny shop in the back lanes. I was interviewed on Radio Carlisle (as it was) by Nigel Holmes in the outside broadcast studio in Penrith. We had to collect the key from The George Hotel. We drove down with my sister as the sunrise lit up the mountains beyond Penrith; I thought this was the most beautiful place on earth. Many books and many radio and TV interviews later, I still remember that moment.

Later, I came back to Cumbria as a guest of Cumbria's Library Service and visited a number of schools including Yewdale in Carlisle. By then readers in Cumbria had fallen in love with Mr Mullett and Napoleon and I still have treasured letters and pictures from Cumbrian schools about the book.

My favourite comment was in a letter from a little lad who must be about 30 now!

"I love Mr Mullett. He's just like my grandad. He's always moaning . . ." he wrote.

And there are folk in Hesket Newmarket who still think Mr Mullett is really Tommy Little, who used to help us with the sheep. Not true, as all the characters are fictional, but the book is based on Caldbeck and the fells around, while that white house up the valley in Mungrisdale might just be the real Home Farm.

A Bolt from the Blue

WHAT A STORM! The thunder rolled and crashed about like marbles on a tin tray. Lightning split the sky and lit up the dark crags with a ghostly light. The rain stung with icy needles.

Mr Mullett and Old Tom, the border collie, were soaked to their skins. All night long they had been out on the fells near Home Farm, looking for sheep, for who could tell where the frightened ewes might have run to in the dark and the rain? Old Tom had trotted tirelessly backwards and forwards herding the poor bedraggled creatures, until every one of them was safely penned near to the farm, for lambing time was close. Mr Mullett had just decided to go home to bed when a terrific crash shook the very ground under his feet. In the same moment a dazzling fork of lightning snaked out of the sky and appeared to hit the farmhouse.

Mr Mullett started to run. Mrs Mullett was in the house all alone. Was the farm on fire? He couldn't see any flames. Perhaps the roof had caved in. It was too dark to see anything through the driving rain.

He reached the yard, and, slipping in his heavy boots, ran across the cobbles to the back door. There was a strange smell in the air; it seemed to be coming from the cow byre and the cows were lowing loudly. But Mr Mullett hadn't time to think of that. He raced up the garden path and burst through the kitchen door.

"Mrs Mullett!" he shouted at the top of his voice. "Mrs Mullett, are you all right?"

"Of course I am!" came a cross voice from under the kitchen table. Mrs Mullett always hid under the kitchen table when there was a storm. The tablecloth was pushed aside and Mrs Mullett and the cat came crawling out.

"But your cows will be in a fine way, if I'm not much mistaken," Mrs Mullett continued, brushing cat hairs off her skirt. "It sounded as if the cow byre was struck by lightning!"

Mr Mullett turned on his heel and half-ran across the farmyard. The strange smell grew stronger. As he approached the byre he pulled up short. He pushed his cap onto the back of his head.

"There's summat wrong here," he said to himself, scratching his head. "It's a black neet right enough. So how is it I can see the byre as clear as day?"

He walked on as cautiously as his great boots would allow. Ahead of him the byre was lit with a strange, flickering light.

"It couldn't be the hay," he said out loud. "It'll not fire, it's that damp." But just in case he picked up a full bucket of rainwater which was standing by the gate. And as he turned the corner an extraordinary sight met his eyes. For there, in all the mud and slush, just beyond the byre, was something lying on the ground.

It was about the shape and size of a rugby football and it pulsed and glowed with a greenish, ghostly light. Mr Mullett ran forward and threw his bucket of water over it. But the thing just went on pulsating and glowing exactly as before. The walls of the cow byre, the pump in the yard, the nose of the tractor sticking out of the barn; all were lit with the same unearthly glow. Mr Mullett shivered.

Very, very cautiously he walked round the thing. He reached the door of the byre and opened it. The cows lowed even louder and kicked sulkily at their stalls. He cushed them until they were quiet. He looked carefully around. There was no fire and no damage. Mr Mullett gave the cows some fresh hay. Then he went out and shut the door firmly behind him. The thing was still sitting in the mud, glowing and flickering in that eerie way. Old Tom was crouching on the far side of it, growling softly with his ears back.

"I think you're right, old lad!" said Mr Mullett to the dog. "This is something for the Ministry man to deal with. Could be giving off rays for all I know. Better keep away from it till morning. Then we'll see about it."

He went back to the kitchen to take off his boots and fell straight to sleep in his chair. Mrs Mullett came in an hour later, as dawn broke, and saw him lying there. Poor old soul! She thought to herself. But he might have taken his boots off! And she went outside to do the milking. She was so sleepy herself that she almost tripped over the thing by the cow byre. By the light of day it looked just like a big stone and not at all frightening.

"Well, bless me!" she exclaimed. "How did that get there?"

She walked round it once and then went to start the milking. But no sooner had she put the pail under the first cow and leaned her grey head against its flank, than Old Tom set up a terrific barking.

"Now what!" she muttered to herself, and she came out of the byre with the milking pail in her hand.

A man was standing by the farm gate. He was quite the most peculiar person Mrs Mullett had ever seen. He wore a

broad-brimmed hat of brightest blue and a long cloak shot through with all the colours of the rainbow. His hair, which grew right down to his waist, was snow white.

The stranger raised his hat.

"Excuse me!" he said in a singsong voice. "Would your husband be in at the moment?"

Mrs Mullett nodded dumbly, opened and shut her mouth a few times by way of experiment, and then, when no sound emerged, turned tail and scampered up the path as fast as her legs would carry her.

Mr Mullett was exceedingly cross at being shaken out of his comfortable sleep.

"Sky-blue hats indeed!" he muttered to himself as he stomped off down the path. "Probably yan o' them cyclepedia salesmen. I'll give him a piece of my mind!"

Mr Mullett was rather taken aback at the extraordinary appearance of the 'cyclepedia salesman.' But he was not going to let on that he was at all surprised. He just fixed the stranger with his steely blue eyes and fished in his pocket for his pipe. There was an uncomfortable silence.

The stranger flushed a delicate shade of pink.

"Forgive me," he said at last. "But I believe you have something of mine." He coughed nervously. "I . . . I dropped it last night on your land."

"I hope, sir," said Mr Mullett sternly, "that you've not bin trespassing on my property!"

The stranger waved his long white hands about in an

agitated fashion.

"Oh, good gracious no! I wouldn't dream . . . dear me! Most embarrassing! How does one explain? I dropped it from above, you see!"

"Out of yan o' them aeroplanes, I suppose!" said Mr Mullett grimly. He had been having a lot of trouble lately from low-flying aircraft frightening his sheep.

"No, no, no!" said the stranger hastily. "One lives in the sky, of course!" he beamed, as though that explained everything.

"Oh aye!" Mr Mullett choked, taking down some smoke the wrong way. He groped for a hanky to wipe his streaming eyes and wondered how long it would take the local police constable, PC Willinsfield, to walk up the fell and subdue a dangerous lunatic.

"You see, it's so very precious to me!" the stranger went on pleadingly.

Mr Mullett's pipe blew out a shower of sparks.

"I'll just go . . . " he began, as he got his breath back. But the stranger was staring fixedly at something beside the cow byre and uttering little moans of joy. Brushing past Mr Mullett, he floated off down the path, his long cloak billowing behind him.

The cows were still bad tempered after their poor night's sleep so when a strange, multicoloured creature came sweeping towards them, making bleating noises to itself and waving its arms about, it was just too much. Instead of queuing in an orderly way to be milked, as they had been doing, they all made a rush for the gate at once. There was a moment when all of them seemed to be stuck in the gateway together. Then there was a splintering noise and an

explosion of cows burst onto the path and thundered into the meadow beyond. Over went Mrs Mullett's milk pail. Mrs Mullett jumped into the cabbage patch and Mr Mullett into the gooseberry bushes. Old Tom leaped onto the henhouse roof, which Mr Mullett said afterwards was a miracle as Old Tom had never jumped that high in his life before, and Mr Mullett had to get a ladder to get him down.

When they had picked themselves up, Mr Mullett looked round for the stranger. He was not feeling too kindly towards him, especially now that he had several long gooseberry spines stuck fast in the seat of his trousers. But then he saw him.

The stranger was sitting in the mud and muck, next to the cow byre. His hat had been trampled in a puddle. His cloak was covered in green slime and he smelt very strongly of cowpats. But he looked wonderfully, marvellously happy, for he clutched the stone which had landed so mysteriously the night before; and in his hands it glowed once more with a magical light.

The stranger struggled to his feet.

"So considerate!" He said in his trilling tone, beaming at Mr Mullett. "Putting it in its own little pen so that the dear creature couldn't run away! So kind!" And he gave the glowing stone an affectionate pat.

Mr Mullett looked round at the remains of the rickety fence which surrounded the cow byre. He pushed back his cap and scratched his head. "Well..." he began.

"How can I ever thank you?" gushed the stranger. "I must repay you! Is there anything . . . anything you need?"

Mr Mullett rubbed the stubble on his chin.

"Well . . . " he began again.

"I insist!" said the stranger gravely. "In any case it's in the rules. Mortals giving assistance to the Gods must be suitably rewarded. Paragraph 728, sub section G, I believe."

"Oh, aye!" said Mr Mullett. Poor lad, he thought to himself. Nutty as a fruit cake. Best humour him.

"Anything! Anything!" repeated the stranger, flinging his arms about in an expansive gesture. A slow smile found its way across Mr Mullett's leathery old face.

"That's reet kind o' ya," he said. "But I think we've got maest things we need, the missus and me. 'Cepting a bit of weather now and then, of course. Any farmer will tell you he could do with a bit of weather! A mite of rain when the land's thirsty and a good patch of sun when the crops want harvesting. Now that isn't much to ask, is it?"

He chuckled at his little joke.

But the stranger clapped his hands with joy, almost forgetting the stone, which began to slip from under his arm.

"The very thing! The very thing! If I can't organise the weather for you, who can?" And he smiled delightedly. "I shall send you Napoleon!"

Mr Mullett's pipe paused halfway to his mouth.

"Napoleon?" he echoed faintly, wishing he had summoned Constable Willinsfield after all. "Who's Napoleon?"

"One of my clouds, of course," explained the stranger airily. "He used to be a General on the Cold Front but, alas, he gets a trifle

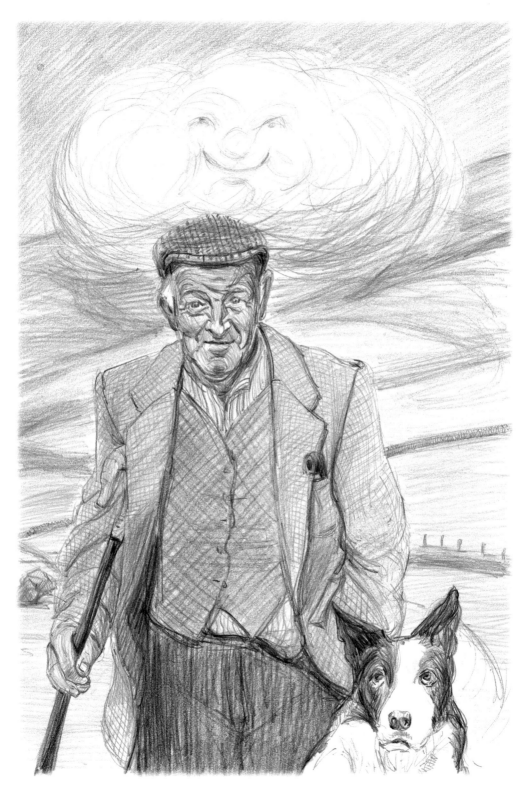

carried away at times - rather impetuous. He would definitely be better off with a smaller patch of sky. I shall send him to you. Consider him a gift. A year's trial to begin with, perhaps? After all, he is a little . . . ahem." Here the stranger paused and glanced skywards anxiously.

"Don't mention it! Farewell! Farewell!" And with a last swirl of his cloak he started off up the fell path.

"Excuse me!" Mr Mullett shouted, his curiosity getting the better of him. The stranger came running lightly back.

"Forgive me asking," said Mr Mullett, "but that stone . . . " he pointed to the object under the stranger's arm, which was still emitting its unearthly green light, ". . . what do you use it for?"

"How silly of me," said the stranger. "It's my thunderbolt, of course. I'm Zeus . . . ahem. King of the Gods, you know, although all that stuff's over and done with now. We're more or less equal now, we Gods and Goddesses, and very well behaved. But they do still let me have my thunderbolt to play with. Here's my card. I shall send Napoleon over tomorrow. Farewell!"

And with that he vanished.

Mr Mullett looked at the space where the stranger's hat had been, where there was now just blue sky and a few fluffy white clouds. He shook his head. Then he looked down at the card in his hand. Like the mysterious stone, it too shone with a magical light, and written on one side, in large letters which shimmered like liquid sunlight, were the words: MR ZEUS.

Mr Mullett turned the card over. On the other side, in slightly smaller letters, it said: 'Olympus, Greece.' But even as he looked

the bright words faded and were gone, and he found himself staring down at an empty white card.

The next day, Mrs Mullett was straining the potatoes in the sink when she heard a peculiar sighing noise. The door opened and shut very gently and suddenly the room seemed to be full of steam.

"Phew!" Mrs Mullett flapped her hand over the potatoes. "I can't see a thing for this blasted steam!" But it only grew thicker and thicker; it was rather like being lost in a dense fog. Mrs Mullett tried to find her way to the door.

All at once a subdued giggling came from the centre of the fog and then a sucking, slurping noise like a watery vacuum cleaner. The steam flew across the room and collected together in a great frothy pile which appeared to be sitting in the rocking chair.

"Oh," gasped Mrs Mullett. "Oh, my goodness!"

The cloud - for such it was - giggled again. It made a noise like water gushing out of a pipe.

"I believe I am expected," it gurgled. "Let me introduce myself. Private Napoleon, Ordinary Cloud, at your service." The cloud sighed. "I was a General once, in charge of a Cold Front. Until a little mix-up in the pressure zones - hardly noticeable really, but they took away my stars all the same . . ." He tailed off sadly and attempted to bow but instead spilled out of the rocking chair onto the floor, where he became involved in a brief struggle with the cat, who, up till now, had been blissfully unaware of all the goings-on.

The cat attempted to bite Napoleon, which was impossible and only gave it hiccups. Mrs Mullett and the cat reached the door of

the kitchen together and there was a brief clash. The cat won. They sprinted neck and neck across the farmyard. The cat disappeared into the barn where it could soothe its ruffled feelings on a mouse or two. Mrs Mullett headed purposefully for Mr Mullett.

Mr Mullett was mending the broken gate post when Mrs Mullett came flying down the path with another of her wild stories. He put down his tools and led her back into the kitchen, where Napoleon, who had found the soap, was lovingly wrapping himself around it until his layers and layers of whiteness were a mass of rainbow bubbles. He looked very beautiful and at intervals he floated gracefully over to the mantelpiece, trailing bubbles as he went, to admire himself in the mirror on the wall.

Mr Mullett took off his cap and then put it back on again. He took 12 matches to light his pipe - a sure sign that he was agitated. He sat down in the rocking chair, which was still a little damp, while Mrs Mullett wondered whether she should offer the cloud a cup of tea, but somehow it didn't seem right. After a bit, she suggested he might like to make himself comfortable on the table. Napoleon thanked her gracefully and arranged his bubbles along the scrubbed deal table, spilling over slightly into the knife drawer. A few stray bubbles floated down onto the stone-flagged floor and paused there for a while before they popped. Each one reflected in its rainbow face the strange scene in the Mullett kitchen: Mr Mullett, with his greasy cap pushed back from his forehead, his old wrinkled face set in a frown, teeth clamped round his pipe; Mrs Mullett with her grey curls all awry, her glasses tipping off the end of her nose, twisting the strings of her pinny and looking extremely nervous.

Only Napoleon, blissfully comfortable on the cool flatness of the table, seemed at all at home. There was an awkward silence, broken only by the sound of Mr Mullett using another four matches to relight his pipe, which had gone out. Then he cleared his throat.

"Tha knaws," he said at last, "I thowt yon Mr Zeus wus some poor off-comer a bit nicked int' head. I nivver took him to heart. If I'd known I was gonna be saddled wid some clood I didn't want, I'd ah told him straight. An' no messin! I'll be a great gowk if I have owt to do wid it!"

Napoleon started to cry and rain fell heavily all over the kitchen floor. At this, Mrs Mullett, who was a motherly sort of person, quite forgot her nerves and said: "There, there!" and tried to mop up Napoleon's tears with her pinny.

The emotion of the moment even overcame Mr Mullett, who went "Hrrmph" and blew his nose. "Perhaps I've been a little hasty," he said awkwardly. "Tha' could stay for a trial period. Come to think of it, yon Zeus character said summat aboot a year's trial. That would suit me as well as owt else. But nobbut a year, nee mair."

Napoleon, tremulous with joy, blew out bubbles in all directions. He swathed himself lovingly around Mr Mullett's head and giggled happily. Mr Mullett's pipe went out with a faint hissing noise. Napoleon withdrew at speed as Mr Mullett started to wheeze in the sudden fog. Mr Mullett sighed and wondered to himself if he wasn't getting a little soft in the head.

"Taking on summat that's no more than a yard of pump watter!" he muttered disgustedly. "To help with t'wedder!

Oh aye! And pigs might fly!"

And he stomped off to finish mending the gate post.

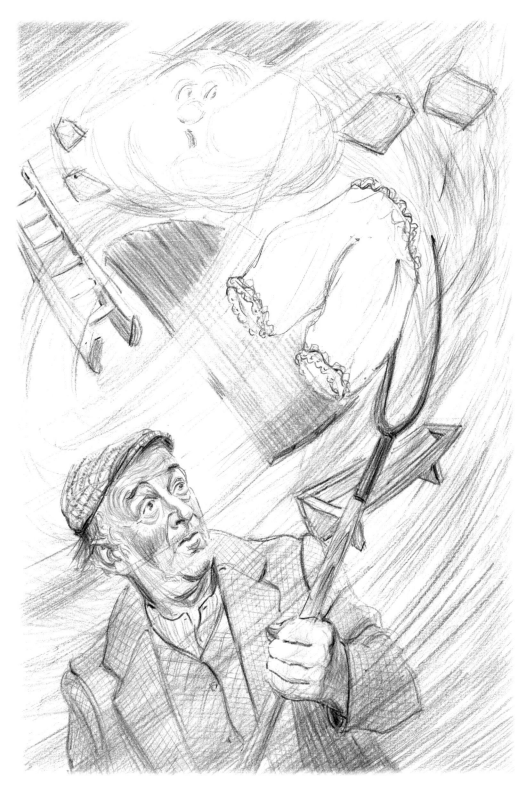

Napoleon whips up a storm

Napoleon knew only too well that Mr Mullett had agreed unwillingly to let him stay for a trial period and that any unfortunate mistakes would provide a good excuse for the cloud to be ejected instantly from Home Farm. So he set to immediately to prove how invaluable he was going to be.

He had been given the job of helping with the weather, so that was what he would do. He would show the Mulletts, as spectacularly as he was able, what a useful cloud he could be. For the first few days he hung close above Mr Mullett listening to his every word. Mr Mullett complained that he had a permanently damp shirt collar, and when he was rash enough to make a casual remark about "t'wedder" the results were dramatic.

On the first morning after Napoleon's arrival he happened to mention that what the ground needed after all the rain was a "gay good wind" to dry it up. Napoleon, filled with zeal, rushed about the sky summoning up his friends on the Old Boy Network and within a very few minutes, just as Mr Mullett was staggering down the intake fields with a huge bundle of hay for the pregnant ewes, a miniature hurricane hit the farm without warning and whipped his precious hay from his grasp and halfway into the next parish before he could draw breath.

No one could deny, an hour later, that the ground was wonderfully dry. Unfortunately it was also littered with tiles,

portions of barn door, a small section of pigsty and a pair of Mrs Mullett's winter bloomers which somehow had become impaled on a pitchfork.

Mr Mullett was a fair man. He recognised that the cloud was trying hard to please. He gritted his teeth, reminded himself of his promise to Napoleon and asked him, as politely as he could manage, whether the cloud could arrange a little sunshine for an hour or two over his winter wheat. Napoleon cleared the sky bossily and stood guard for the rest of the day while the sun beat down and the rabbits, thinking that Spring had come at last, came out for a quiet nibble at the young shoots.

Mr Mullett sighed with relief, went off to retrieve his ladder from his unhelpful neighbour Mr Sourworthy, and had the embarrassment of trying to explain why it was resting in the topmost branches of his apple tree.

Napoleon was even more of a liability inside. Whichever way the Mulletts turned they seemed to be in a permanent fog, so that they scarcely knew whether they were on their heads or their heels. Napoleon was a very affectionate cloud and extremely curious about everything - the strange nature of the round objects which both Mr and Mrs Mullett occasionally wore on the ends of their noses, for instance. He discovered that if he looked through one of the round things, it made everything bigger. It was the same whether he was on the outside looking in, or the inside looking out. So it was that Mr and Mrs Mullett found their spectacles were permanently steamed up, and when Mrs Mullett twice tripped over the cat and Mr Mullett had walked smack into the door jamb,

Napoleon was given a sharp dressing down by Mr Mullett and went off to sulk in the dairy.

Then there were Mr Mullett's pockets. What a strange exotic smell came from those dark, tweedy cavities! A rich mixture of pipe tobacco and cattle concentrate with just a whiff of foot rot powder thrown in. Mr Mullett kept an old leather tobacco pouch in his pocket, with a thin slice of potato inside to keep the tobacco moist. On the morning after Napoleon had explored Mr Mullett's pockets, his tobacco was very moist indeed! Squelchy might have been a better word to describe it.

Napoleon seemed to spend a great deal of time sulking in the dairy. What with the fog and the mist and the steam, and the sudden blast of hail when he passed too close to the open refrigerator, and the way he draped himself so inconveniently in a slolloping sort of way all over the kitchen table - occasionally shutting his extremities in the knife drawer - it all became a bit too much.

Tempers grew rather short. But it was quiet and cool in the dairy, and Napoleon could doze in peace on the marble slab where Mrs Mullett made her butter and cheese. In fact, only there did his presence seem to be properly appreciated.

"He'll be worth his weight in gold come the summer," commented Mrs Mullett delightedly a few days after Napoleon's arrival. "I can't mind when I've ever made better butter! Whatever his faults, he does keep everywhere so deliciously cool and moist. You mark my words," she nodded over her knitting, "he'll be worth his weight in gold!"

Mr Mullett looked up reluctantly from his contemplation of the

fat stock prices in *The Cumberland News* and muttered: "Since he weighs all but nowt, that won't make us very rich!"

Mrs Mullett sighed and went on with her knitting. Napoleon, pretending to be dozing in the rocking chair, squinted cautiously at Mr Mullett. The farmer, he decided, looked a little sour. He did not have quite that joyful glow about him that Napoleon would have expected of anyone who had just been given a present by the King of the Gods.

The cloud began to feel a trifle nervous. Mr Zeus had said a year's trial, but did that mean he could be sent back at any time if he disgraced himself? Napoleon did not think he could stand any more disgraces. A shiver ran through him as he remembered the terrible moment when Mr Zeus had demoted him to Private, when the awful truth had finally come to light about who, in the middle of the holiday season, had caused a blizzard over the Scilly Isles lasting for 17 days and nights. The humiliation! He could hardly bear to think of it!

If Napoleon had any teeth, he would undoubtedly have gritted them. I'll show them! He thought. I'll show them I can be useful! And wanted! And loved, he added in a wave of self pity.

He stole another look at Mr Mullett. Yes, there was no doubt about it. The farmer definitely had the look of someone who has had the top of his egg pinched. Had he behaved so badly since his arrival? Napoleon wondered. True, he had sat on the fire, a singeing experience for a sensitive cloud, and undeniably the fire which, after belching clouds of black smoke over Mr Mullett's plate of ham and eggs, had gone out. True, he had sneaked under the bonnet of the

Land Rover for a quick nap and, according to Mr Mullett (although Napoleon was doubtful on this point), he had so dampened the plugs that it had refused to start; as a result of which Mr Mullett had been late for the ram sales and missed buying a prize tup. But was it his fault? Life could be a little unfair at times.

Mr Mullett folded his newspaper carefully and rose to his feet.

"I'm just garn up t'fell to see Jed," he said to Mrs Mullett. His wife was counting the stitches on her knitting, but she nodded and smiled. Mr Mullett took his cap down from its nail by the door, pulled on his boots and struggled into the old tweed jacket which was the most he ever wore even on the worst of nights out on the fell. He opened the kitchen door and a wall of driving snow was lit for a moment in the lamplight.

"There's a bit of a squall!" he said equably. "I'd best tek t'torch."

Napoleon had glimpsed the snow for himself and felt the icy blast of wind as Mr Mullett opened the door. But when Old Tom (the collie dog) slipped from his accustomed place by the fire and made to go with his master, Napoleon was not to be outdone.

As soon as he was out of the door, he regretted it, for the wind nearly tore him apart, and by the time they had battled down the fell path an urge rather like the desire to sneeze spread over him. At the door of the little cottage where Mr Mullett stopped and knocked, he delivered a modest little snow shower of his own on the farmer's head. It was a pity that everywhere else it had stopped snowing several minutes before. Mr Mullett looked up with a long-suffering expression and, taking off his cap, banged it with unnecessary violence against his boot. Napoleon was hurt.

The door of the cottage opened, and a wizened old man peered out.

"Oh, it's Mr Mullett!" he said. "I've bin expecting yer. Come on in and have a cup o' tea."

Napoleon, slipping in behind Mr Mullett and Old Tom, felt that no one would notice him there. The air was heavy with peat smoke and only a flickering oil lamp lit the scene. In front of the glowing fire stood a cardboard box.

"It's a young hogget," said the old man, bending down he lifted a tiny black lamb out of the box. "Atkinson down at Emblethwaite . . . he brought it up 'ere. I've been givin' it the pap." And he produced a baby's bottle still half full of milk.

Napoleon was enchanted and, forgetting his wish to remain unnoticed, floated forward from his dark corner by the door and hovered over the tiny lamb. The little creature looked up and, seeing Napoleon's soft white fluffiness suspended above, opened its mouth and gave a weak "Maa . . ."

Napoleon dropped lower. The lamb snuffled the moist, tingly edges of the cloud, sneezed once or twice, and, with another happy "Maa . . .", closed its eyes and went to sleep.

Jed did not seem at all surprised to see Napoleon. He gave a quiet chuckle.

"Now would yer look

at that," he said softly. "The young 'un thinks it's his mother. He'll be in gay good fettle now."

He leaned forward and stoked up the fire, putting the blackened kettle onto the hob over the flames.

"So thoos got thisell a cloud, then," he said after a few minutes. Mr Mullett grunted. "I've always wanted a cloud misell," the old man went on. "Being a shepherd up on t'fell, tha knows. Clouds and sheep! Clouds and sheep fer company, and my dog Bess. I couldn't ask for mair." Mr Mullett shook his head.

"There's many'll think I'm a great gowk!" he replied. "Either that or they'll think I'm mekking it aw up!"

The shepherd chuckled.

"Aye, there's not many'll believe tha, that's reet enough. And tha should be grateful for that. As for misell, I've seen too many mysteries up on t'fells to be surprised at owt."

"Aye," agreed Mr Mullett. "It's a strange place up there. And some funny folk."

And he told the shepherd the whole story, while the kettle hissed on the fire and Napoleon, cuddled up to the sleeping lamb, sang to it about its mother.

"Well," said the shepherd when he had finished. "It's a strange story, but tha's reet enough. There are some funny folk up on t'fell."

The old man picked up the steaming kettle with a piece of rag and filled a teapot which stood ready on the hearth.

"Does tha want me on t'farm tomorrow?" he asked.

Mr Mullett nodded. "That's why I cem," he said. "Will thoo come up and stay for t'lambing?"

Jed rubbed his hands together and chuckled. "Looks as though we'll have good weather for it!"

Mr Mullett peered out of the window where the snow lay diagonally across the pane.

"I've brought sheep right doon into t'intake fields," he said. "After t'storm t'other night and then the snow coming, I'll keep them off t'fell."

They were soon deep in conversation about lambing.

It was very late when Mr Mullett finally said goodbye to Jed. And as he opened the door, he saw that the snow lay deep on the path.

"Lend us a shovel," he called, and between them they cleared a way to the gate.

"Snow's drifting again!" he muttered. "I'd best get back and check the sheep."

They made their slow way up the fell, Mr Mullett feeling for the track with his stick and Old Tom running ahead to see if it was safe. Napoleon floated overhead in the frosty sky beneath the spangling stars. The snow had stopped falling. Everywhere was silent. A little owl ke-wicked into the dark. The cloud was cold but happy.

Mr Mullett reached the farm gate and stopped. He pushed his cap back on his head and looked up at Napoleon. For the first time, the sour look he usually reserved for Napoleon appeared to have left his face.

"You did a right good job on that young hogget!" he remarked. "I can't say I think you're any great shakes at controlling the weather, but you'll be a gay good mother to orphan lambs.

Now all we have to teach you is how to give milk!"

There was a pause. Then suddenly, pealing out across the frosty fells, there came the summer sound of water burbling and bubbling. It was Napoleon laughing.

During the next few weeks Napoleon's life came to be dominated by lambs. When Jed arrived to stay for the lambing, he brought the little black lamb, who recognised Napoleon immediately and refused his bottle until the cloud wrapped his white fluffiness about the box. Mrs Mullett complained that it was very difficult trying to plug a lamb onto a bottle in the middle of a thick fog, but Jed chuckled and said: "Thoo can give 'em milk, but thoo can't be their mother too. Thoo'll have to leave that to yon clood!"

After that Napoleon spent his time in the kitchen surrounded by lambs. More and more started to arrive, each in its own cardboard box filled with warm straw. Mrs Mullett, her hands red and swollen from the cold, seemed to do nothing but feed greedy mouths with endless bottles. A large number of triplets had been born that year and not all the mothers could cope with three lambs suckling at once. Then there were the lambs who had lost their mothers, and lambs whose mothers had refused to let them feed. Napoleon found himself stretched thinner and thinner as he spread himself over the growing number of cardboard boxes, giving comfort to each lamb.

It had been much easier being a General on the Cold Front!

And when Mrs Mullett ran out of space in the kitchen and lit a fire in the parlour to accommodate yet more lambs, Napoleon felt

that if he stretched himself any more he would definitely go twang, and there would be nothing left of him except a few tendrils of mist.

But then, at last, the Lamb Bank got under way. Every morning, Jed and Mr Mullett listened to the radio while they were demolishing a mountainous breakfast of fat bacon, sausages, eggs and a vast plate of "poddish" made out of oatmeal, to keep out the cold. The BBC local radio station broadcast a special programme each day where farmers could ring in if they had a spare ewe which had lost her lambs, or orphan lambs who needed a foster mother, and in this way the two could be cleverly matched together. So, soon – to everyone's relief –the number of cardboard boxes in the kitchen and the parlour began to grow fewer, until suddenly, miraculously, the sun started to shine, the snow melted, green grass bloomed fresh in the meadows and the lambs in the barn were allowed outside for the first time since they had been born.

On that first spring day, Mr Mullett stood by the gate of the intake field, drawing the first good smoke from his pipe for three weeks and listening to that heart-lifting chorus of lambs calling to their mothers and mothers scolding their lambs for straying too far. Mrs Mullett came out of the kitchen with the last cardboard box and set it down just inside the field. In it was Jed's little black lamb.

She lifted it out of the box. It tottered about for a few seconds, uncertain on its nobbly legs. The field was dotted with Herdwick ewes and their lambs, but it seemed that nowhere was there a mother for the black lamb. It gave a frightened "Maa" as it looked around. The world was so big and bright and thoroughly unfriendly. Then, suddenly, a familiar cloud swooped out of the blue sky.

The lamb tottered forward and, as the cloud skimmed down to ground level, it plunged happily into its own particular fog.

Mrs Mullett drew on his pipe and puffed out a miniature cloud of his own. He nodded to Napoleon, his eyes twinkling.

"Seems thoo'll have to stay for a while yet, lad!" he commented.

Then he stomped off to the house for a well-earned sleep.

The Carrowdale Sop
gets really nasty!

Napoleon was not popular for long. The black lamb at last attached itself to a huge Herdwick ewe who was too absent-minded to notice how many lambs were suckling beneath her. The cloud's brief moment of glory as a substitute mother was over. Spring had arrived on a warm, bracken-scented breeze. Daffodils burst into life. Buds sprang open at the touch of the sun. Lambs gambolled. Chicks hacked their way out of their shells. Beaks were stuffed full of worms. Everywhere there was a burgeoning of grass and tree and crop. Napoleon felt out of it. He became bored and a little restless.

He took to trailing theatrically behind Mr Mullett as he inspected every corner of the farm. The farmyard witnessed scenes of Napoleon scattering dew across the morning grass, Napoleon draped fetchingly among the cherry blossom, Napoleon flushed with pink at sunset. It was all a bit much. Mr Mullett was reminded of the extravagant film stars who always seemed to be drifting down marble staircases and to whom Mrs Mullett had been much addicted when they were courting. Mr Mullett was not impressed.

"Aye," he muttered one morning after he had found that the spring which fed the intake fields had dried up another three inches overnight in the drought. "Thoo might think thoo looks like t'young tup that's prettied oop for t'show, but just thoo remember, lad,

many a good topcoat covers a gay shabby suit!"

Napoleon blushed.

"That Mr Zeus of yours," Mr Mullett went on in the same aggrieved tone. "He tells me thoos come to help wid t'weather! And now, when I need a spot of rain, all yer can deur is prance aboot like a steg on a het girdle!"

Napoleon was deeply stung. Steg was the Cumbrian word for gander. Napoleon had an intense and lasting dislike of geese generally, after Mr Mullett's prize gander had hissed him into the corner of the barn and trapped him there for an hour. Right! He thought petulantly. And without further ado he proceeded to raise the level of the brook to the point where, if Mr Mullett had still been standing on the bank, instead of hot-footing it back to the farmhouse shouting Cumbrian curses and wringing out his cap, he would probably have been washed away.

Relations between Mr Mullett and his cloud were a little strained after that. The drought continued, but Napoleon steadfastly refused to rain again, feeling that his efforts were not appreciated. In the end Mr Mullett gave up trying to persuade him and was careful not to make any reference to the weather when Napoleon was overhead, which he usually was. Looking grey and dejected, the cloud followed Mr Mullett wherever he went, saying nothing but managing always to get in the way.

And so it went on, until things finally came to a head during the sheep shearing. After Mr Mullett had spent 10 frustrating minutes in the hot sun shearing Napoleon instead of the rather puzzled sheep he was holding between his legs, the farmer expressed the

opinion that Napoleon would be better employed on top of Mount Everest, or in some other distant location. Or, failing that, he suggested in no uncertain terms that Napoleon take himself off to the top of the fell and stay there!

Napoleon drifted away in a huff, but he never got as far as the fell. Instead, he spent the night hanging about miserably above the farm, soaked in self pity. In the morning, however, his attention was caught by an extraordinary amount of activity that seemed to be going on in the intake fields below.

The cloud could just make out the stick figures of Jed and Mr Mullett standing by one of the gates, harrying sheep through in a long stream. Napoleon could hear faint splashing sounds and he was intensely curious. If he was careful, he reckoned that in all the excitement he would hardly be noticed. He slipped down swiftly into the field below and mingled with the sheep which were still waiting to go through the gate.

Jed was standing on the other side of the dry stone wall, counting aloud in the old Cumbrian way, as each sheep came past.

"Yan, tyan, tethera, methera, pimp," he said steadily. "Sethera, lethera, hovera, dovera, dick. Yan-a-dick, tyan-a-dick, tethera-a-dick, methera-a-dick, bumfit. Yan-a-bumfit, tyan-a-bumfit, tethera-a-bumfit, methera-a-bumfit, gigot."

Each time he got to 20, he would put a finger up and start again. When he had a handful of fingers up, he took a round pebble out of his pocket and put it on the wall, because that meant he had reached a hundred.

Napoleon was fascinated. He knew about ordinary counting,

from listening to Mrs Mullett counting her stitches – one, two, three – in front of the fire, but this counting was almost like a song. He wreathed himself around the nearest ewe as she approached the gate. There was a bit of a crush. Napoleon found himself in imminent danger of being trampled into wisps, when suddenly Jed reached out his crook and hauled Napoleon's ewe at top speed through the gateway.

Napoleon could hear the splashing ahead of him. Whatever was going on, he had to know! The next second he saw red. There was red in every particle of him. It was foul! He could see nothing but a red haze. Where was he? Then slowly, daylight seeped in around him like a reluctant dawn. He looked back, but before he had time to see what had caused the red, he found himself being shaken violently by the sheep he had so unwisely wrapped himself around. Shreds of Napoleon, tinged with pink, floated up into the blue and hastily tried to collect themselves together, like a man in a funny film who has just had his trousers blown off.

The sheep which Jed and Mr Mullett had so thoroughly dunked in the sheep dip maa-ed loudly and then went scampering off up the fell. Napoleon, a tattered-looking rag of a cloud, finally disentangled himself and trailed after her, spilling disinfected rain on the bracken as he went.

Mr Mullett leaned over the gate and watched Napoleon's departure. An expression of disbelief passed briefly across the furrows of his face and he shook his head slowly.

"That clood'll have to ga!" he said finally and jammed his pipe back between his teeth with considerable force, as though that were

the end of the matter. Jed went on counting to himself. Only a slight shaking of his shoulders showed that he was moved at all.

Napoleon's pride was very shaken. He could not bring himself to go back to the home farm, where his pinkish, raggedy appearance would undoubtedly cause much merriment. He decided to find a cave and sulk.

He drooped on up the fell. Soon Home Farm was only a tiny grey rectangle surrounded by the grey-walled fields. Napoleon had not been up so high since he had first come to the farm on that bitter February day. A pang of homesickness ran through him. He rained a bit more disinfectant onto a passing rabbit, who was stuck with the smell for days and banished from the warren.

The tussocky grass grew sparser and vanished altogether. The hill path, which Napoleon had been unconsciously following, grew steeper and steeper. Vast walls of granite brooded in shadow. A buzzard mewed from the crag top. An icy wind whipped round the curve of the fell. Then Napoleon saw the walker.

The young man had obviously been following a path round the bend in the fell. But as he came round the corner and the valley opened out before him, he must have realised that what he had been following so faithfully was only a sheep track after all and one which petered out on the steepest part of the fell. As Napoleon watched from above, he started trying to scramble back up the steeply swelling crag. But after the harsh winter, the rock was in a dangerous condition - there was a thick covering of damp moss and a mass of scree. And suddenly Napoleon and the walker found themselves in a thick, dank, grey mist. The walker, panicked by the

change in the weather, missed his footing and rolled over and over down the steep side of the fell.

Napoleon struggled helplessly in the grip of the heavy grey cumulus. The same suffocating feeling came over him as he felt when there was a grey cap hanging over Skiddaw, and bad weather was on the way.

"Well, well, well! If it isn't Napoleon!" A sneering voice sounded from somewhere within the huge cloud. "Once a General, now a tatty bit of dishclout!"

A frisson of fear ran through Napoleon. It was the Carrowdale Sop, the meanest, nastiest cloud in the whole of Lakeland. He recalled in a flash the saying which Jed had repeated a few weeks before:

No matter if 'tis summer's day
There's mucky weather on the way
If on fell top
Thoo spots Carrowdale Sop!

And, as if to echo Jed's words, without further warning large soft flakes of snow began to fall.

"Wait! Wait!" shouted Napoleon, struggling desperately against the terrible pull of the cloud around him, which seemed to be about to take him apart and swallow him. "You don't understand! There's an injured walker down there. He's fallen on the fell. We've got to help him, keep him warm. Please, please let the sunshine back!"

The dark cloud quivered with menace.

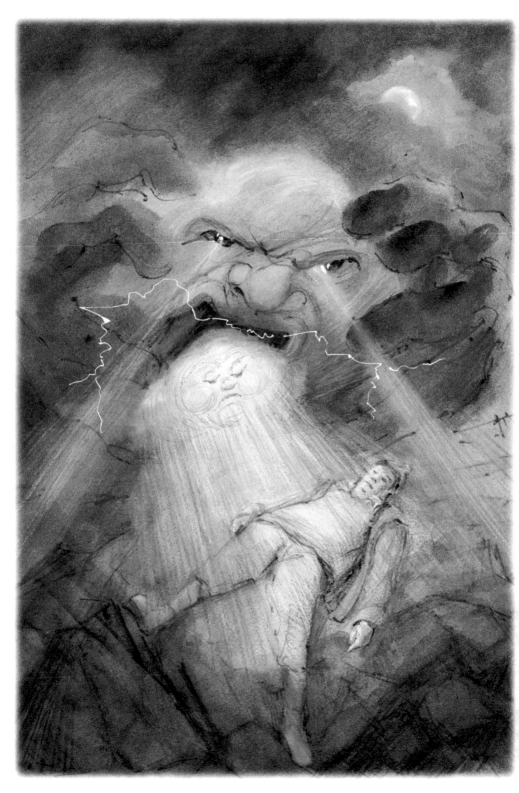

"Folk should know better than to walk alone, without a map. They should know that I lurk in the fells even on the sunniest day, ready to bring winter down on them. Men are fools and they should pay for it!" And the Carrowdale Sop crackled with electric laughter.

Napoleon felt himself growing weaker and weaker. Gradually, the powerful cumulus was eating him up. Soon he would be no more.

But suddenly there came a sharp explosive sound from within the great cloud. And then another. The cumulus was shaken by spasms of giant coughing. It began to fall apart. Fragments of it flew in all directions. Napoleon heard bits of voices coming from all round.

"Ergh! What is that disgusting stuff? Ergh! You're trying to poison me! Ergh!" Gradually the voices became fainter and fainter and more and more fragmented. Sunlight streamed down from a blue sky. Only the faint receding wisps of mist which floated up the fell gave a clue that here, a few moments before, had been the fearful Carrowdale Sop. And as the sunlight broke through upon the fell, light dawned on Napoleon's cloudy mind. It was the sheep dip! The Carrowdale Sop had tried to eat him up but had ended up swallowing a mouthful of Mr Mullett's anti-tick mixture.

Napoleon examined his edges. There was not too much harm done. And he was a brilliant glowing white once more. The Carrowdale Sop must have absorbed all that awful pinkish stuff. Well, at least, even if the terrible cumulus ever managed to reform itself, people would be able to see it coming for miles!

Napoleon swooped at top speed over the fell towards the spot where he had seen the young walker slip. There he was! He had fallen about 50 feet on to a little mossy plateau. He was very still. What if he were dead? A shiver of horror passed through Napoleon. He plunged down until he was hovering a few feet above the figure. What could he do?

The walker opened his eyes and looked up at the agitated, swirling shape which hung above him. That's it! he thought. I'm dead and gone to heaven! Napoleon, shooting out strange abstract appendages as he struggled against the updraught which threatened to push him skywards once again, managed to lower himself further.

"Are you an angel?" enquired the young man in a weak voice.

Napoleon blushed.

"Not quite!" he answered with becoming modesty. "Actually, I think you're alive!"

"Alive!" echoed the young man in amazement. He tried to stand up. There was an agonising pain in his leg and it wouldn't work. Perhaps he was alive after all. He was sure you wouldn't feel pain in heaven.

"I can't stand up!" he said weakly, closing his eyes.

Napoleon looked at the blue sky above him, and the sun shining down. He hoped it would last.

"I'm going to get help," he whispered, floating close to the walker's ear. "When you feel a bit better, try to cover yourself with bracken. You can reach it if you lean carefully across the ledge. It'll keep you warm."

The young man nodded dumbly. He really was not feeling at all well. It would be lovely to go to sleep here on the ledge.

"And keep awake!" A scream like an express train in his ear woke him with a start. Then the cloud wisped away out of sight.

Napoleon had a struggle to get down to the valley. Warm air currents were gusting up from the valley floor into the colder air above. It was against his very nature to go down instead of up. Fortunately, he was helped by a freak down-draught from between the crags. But as he dropped lower and lower, and his coldness met the warm air below him, he found himself bubbling and churning inside most uncomfortably.

He still had not quite adjusted his temperature when he arrived at Home Farm. There was no one about in the fields or in the yard. Mr Mullett was having his dinner. Napoleon poured in through the kitchen skylight. Mr Mullett, Jed and Mrs Mullett were finishing off an enormous tatie-pot which had been simmering on the range all morning.

Napoleon bobbed anxiously over the table. Mr Mullett, knife and fork pointing skywards, was holding forth about the scandalous price he had been getting in the market for weaners. Jed was saying "Aye" every few minutes with his mouth full. Mrs Mullett, who was in charge of pigs, was butting in as well. None of them noticed Napoleon. He was nearly exploding with anxiety. In his mind was a picture of what would happen to the young man if it began to snow again, if the Carrowdale Sop should come back, if the walker should fall asleep and tumble off the ledge. He could stand it no longer.

A high pitched scream – this time more like two express trains – rent the air and simultaneously a light shower ruined the remains of the tatie-pot (though that was an accident). Mr Mullett leapt out of his chair as though he had been shot, dropping his knife and fork; the cat jumped on to the table and knocked over a jug of cream and a dish of bottled plums; and Jed and Mrs Mullett banged heads as they both tried to remove the cat.

Napoleon had certainly succeeded in getting their attention. It was, however, several seconds before everyone stopped hurling insults (and in Mrs Mullett's case, the dishcloth) at the cloud and was prepared to listen. But as soon as Napoleon had gabbled out an explanation Mr Mullett grabbed his cap, slammed into the Land Rover and screeched out of the yard, heading for Carrowbridge and the police station. Within minutes of his getting there, the nearest Mountain Rescue Team was on its way to the bottom of the fell with an ambulance.

Meanwhile, Mrs Mullett had found two warm blankets, a flask of hot tea and a bottle of brandy which Jed quickly loaded into a rucksack. Soon he was loping with his easy shepherd's stride up the fell path with Napoleon leading the way.

The young walker had managed to stretch across to the rock wall and pluck some bracken. He was grateful for the covering – a thin wind was stirring in the fells, a wind with a cold cutting edge like a knife. The walker shivered. He ached all over from his bruises and his leg was numb. If only he could sleep for a little while. He remembered the cloud's warning "Keep awake!" and he snapped his eyes open. Cloud? What was that about a cloud?

A cloud had spoken to him – he was sure of it! No, he must have been dreaming. Anyway, he was too tired to care any more.

The walker slept. Slowly, imperceptibly, he began to tip forward down the slope of the ledge. His hand relaxed on the clump of bracken he had been holding. There was nothing to stop him falling now.

"Gan ahint!" The cry came from high up on the fell. The next moment Jed's sheepdog, Bess, leapt on to the ledge from above and fastened her teeth into the young man's coat. He blinked awake, in time to see a surprisingly agile old man with a rucksack on his back climb down onto the ledge. And hovering a few feet above him was that cloud again.

Constable Willinsfield walked up the fell path that evening to tell the Mulletts that all was well with the young walker and that he would be out of hospital in a few days.

"He had a crack with our sergeant," said the constable, taking off his cap and wiping his brow. "And, do you know, he sent back a gay strange message. I can't puzzle it oot. He said to thank the clood for saving his life. Now wouldn't you think he was a bit nicked in the heed, saying a thing like that?"

At that moment, Constable Willinsfield became aware of a low rumbling noise. It seemed to come from behind a long line of jars and pots, which Mrs Mullett had been in the process of filling up in readiness for Carrowbridge Fair the following week. Every time the low rumbling noise came forth, the jars chinked together in a sort of advanced harmony. The result was quite pleasing, but it had the effect of making the constable profoundly uneasy.

There it was again! Trrr, Trrr, chink, chink! The whole table was vibrating. The remaining hairs on Constable Willinsfield's scalp began to stand on end. For there, on the far side of the scrubbed deal table, was a huge white frothy mass which was unquestionably the source of the rumbling noise. Every time that Napoleon snored, he trembled like a giant blancmange.

If there had been a world record for stout constables running down fells, Constable Willinsfield would probably have broken it. And all the way down he muttered: "Folk said yon farmer had a clood. I nivver would have believed it, but happen they're reet!"

Napoleon was very, very tired. He had had enough of adventures for the time being. He had even had enough of being a hero. He just went on snoring softly on the kitchen table, while Mrs Mullett got on with potting preserves for the Women's Institute tent at the Fair and tried not to notice that Napoleon was wobbling the table so much that the occasional dollop of rhubarb preserve was falling into the chutney.

Hot air at the fair!

The week before Carrowbridge Fair was always one of the busiest times on the farm. Mr and Mrs Mullett only ever took two days' holiday in the year – one for the Women's Institute outing to Silcombe Bay and one for the Carrowbridge Fair – so there was much excitement as well as plenty of preparation. Mrs Mullett was finishing off her jams and pickles and was busy bringing her early peas and carrots to final glory for the Gardening Society competitions. Mr Mullett had his hands full grooming his beasts for the stock classes. He would be competing against the best in Cumberland and it was important for every farmer to show his animals in top condition.

Everyone was so preoccupied that Napoleon felt thoroughly neglected. No one seemed to remember how hard he had worked on Mrs Mullett's vegetable garden; a touch of sun here and a light shower there had brought the vegetables to something resembling the pictures on the fronts of the seed packets – perfection indeed! No one seemed to care that he kept the grass lush in the end pasture so that the coats of the young heifers were as glossy as newly-blacked boots. Now, when he made himself at home on the kitchen table, Mrs Mullett complained that he was steaming the labels off the jampots. Then she said some rather hurtful things when he got tangled in a sack of flour and dusted the cat white. The cat was even more unpleasant about it, and as Napoleon floated out across the

yard, he nursed a rather tattered area around his rear where the cat's claws had raked away at his edges.

But Napoleon forgot his grievances when at last the great day came. What a lot there was to do! Mr and Mrs Mullett had both been up since before dawn. There were still animals to be fed, cows to milk, eggs to be collected – the everyday chores of the farm which could never be overlooked, as well as the hole which had suddenly appeared in one of the stone walls, through which sheep would get into the young barley if it were not fixed straight away.

With all this activity going on Napoleon was as excited as anyone. He floated over the cow byre where Mr Mullett was giving his beasts a last spit and polish. The prize heifer, Pride of the Fells, was having her hooves trimmed. She looked at Napoleon suspiciously and rolled her eyes at him. Napoleon thought she looked rather miserable. He determined to cheer her up.

"Whoo!" he went, in his very best ghost imitation.

Crack! went the heifer's hoof as it made contact with Mr Mullett's shin. Mr Mullett said a few shockingly bad words under his breath and a lot more out loud to Napoleon. The cloud rose rapidly into the sky, feeling very offended.

He received no warmer a welcome when the time came to leave. Jed had volunteered to drive the truck, so Mr and Mrs Mullett squeezed into the Land Rover along with baskets of peas and carrots, a box full of jars (the jams and pickles), Mr Mullett's best stockman's coat and Wellingtons, a huge trifle which Mrs Mullett was entering for the Women's Institute Desserts and Mr Mullett's prize tup, who started off in the back of the Land Rover but twice

pushed his great curly horns over the seat in an effort to eat the trifle.

So when Napoleon began to pour in through the open window on the driver's side he was very unpopular indeed. And that was why the little convoy of Jed in the truck and Mr and Mrs Mullett in the Land Rover, winding down the long track to the town below, had a sulky-looking cloud following behind, who coughed occasionally from the dust in a self-pitying sort of way and muttered about the hard-heartedness of farmers in general and Mr Mullett in particular.

When they reached the Fair, by the time Mrs Mullett had placed her entries in the appropriate tents and Mr Mullett had checked in for the stock classes, a crowd had begun to gather on the main lawn for the Grand Opening. This was to be performed, this year as every year, by Lady Marchbank of Carrowbridge Hall.

The platform party took their seats. The Chairman of the District Council rose to give a speech of welcome. He began by remarking how fortunate they were this year with the weather and glanced upwards to what had been up till then a cloudless blue sky. For at that moment a rather sulky-looking cloud appeared and hung purposefully over the heads of the crowd. Napoleon was searching for Mr Mullett.

"Yes," continued the Chairman, "as long as that nasty little cloud goes away, I'm sure we shall have a very fine day indeed."

Napoleon was mortally offended.

"Nasty little cloud, indeed!" he rumbled to himself. "The cheek of it! I've a good mind to rain on them just to teach them a lesson!"

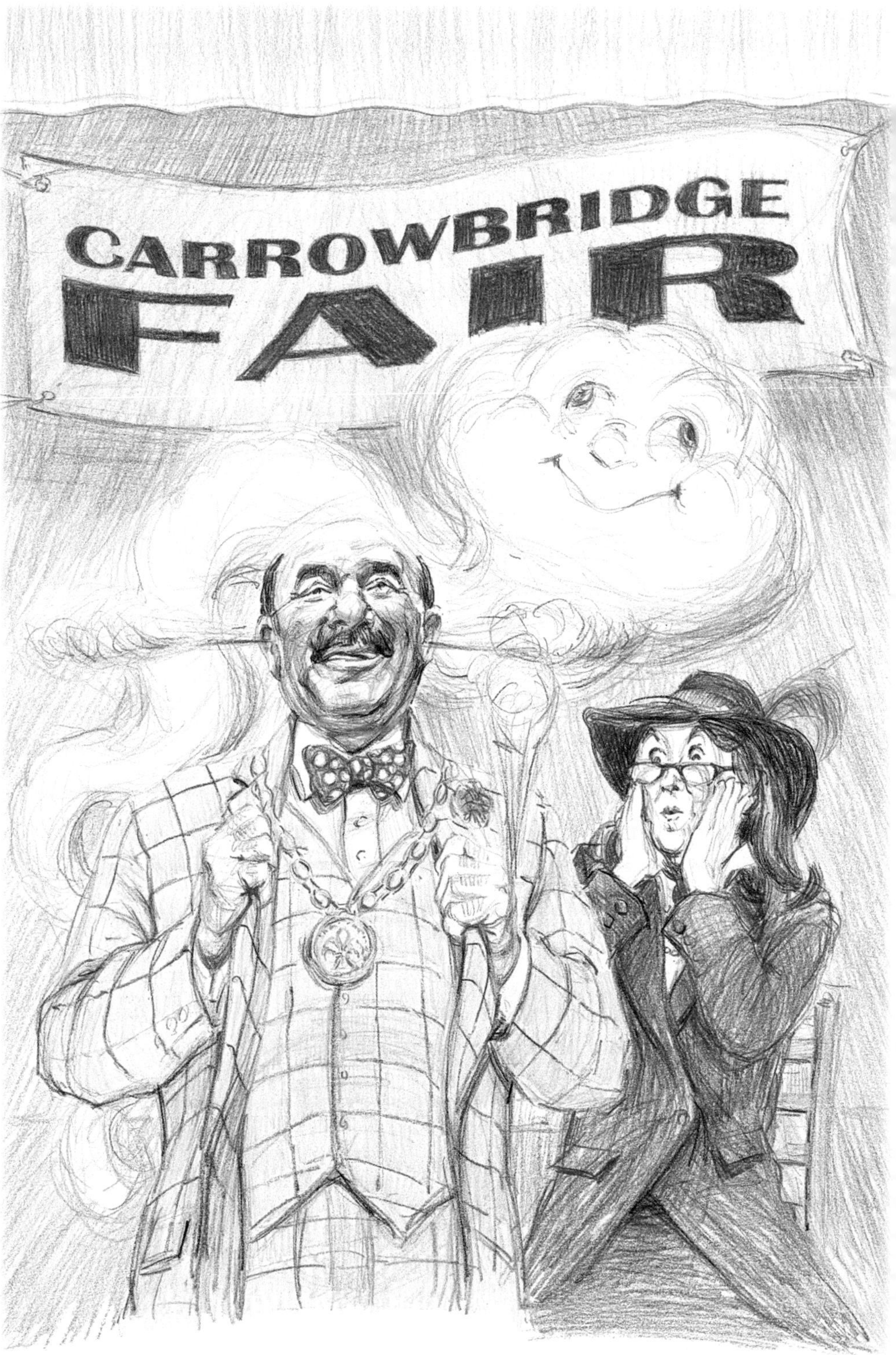
CARROWBRIDGE
FAIR

But although Napoleon was often mischievous, he was never unkind, and he had set his heart on making the day a very special one for the Mulletts.

But suddenly he felt a sprackling round his edges, and, glancing upwards, felt his insides turn to water. A few layabout clouds, who as usual had nothing better to do, had spotted Napoleon and decided to join him. They clustered above him, giggling sillily.

"Thinking of having a bit of a shower?" asked one of them. "Mind if we join you?"

"Go away!" hissed Napoleon. "Can't you see there's a Fair going on!"

But the clouds only laughed all the more and hugged each other with glee. And, as they hugged each other, they grew denser and denser and darker and darker. People began to glance skywards anxiously and wish they had brought their umbrellas. The Chairman stopped talking, and as the first spots of rain began to fall, the platform party, as well as almost all of the listening crowd, made a dash for the beer tent.

"No!" shouted Napoleon. But the layabout clouds were having a wonderful time. They started to rain in earnest on the fleeing crowd.

But not everyone was running, for there, right in the middle of the grass, still as a stone, stood Mr Mullett with his nose in his programme, totally absorbed in the lists of stock classes. He did not seem to have noticed that everyone had left or that he was getting wet through.

"Four heifers to Ring One for the first class," he muttered,

counting on his fingers. "And Dawston Lad to the Tup Class at twelve o'clock."

He scratched his head.

"I'll nivver do it!" he moaned to himself. A drip ran down his nose and landed on the programme, smudging the print. Another galloped skittishly down the back of his neck. Mr Mullett looked up.

All he could see was Napoleon hovering anxiously overhead. He could not see the layabout clouds, which were raining straight through Napoleon. "You great gowk!" Mr Mullett exploded. "Thoos rained on me and all t'fowks at t'fair. You gormless, sackless dummel heed!"

Napoleon had no idea what a dummel-head was, but he was pretty sure it wasn't very nice. Feeling desolate, he watched Mr Mullett stomp off to the show ring in a fury. The layabout clouds, tired of their game, slouched away at last in search of fresh mischief. The sun shone down on the wet fields, making everything sparkle. Steam rose from the benches. The platform party emerged from the beer tent and the Chairman of the District Council began his speech all over again.

It had been a very boring speech the first time round; it was even worse the second. The Chairman told a few jokes. Nobody laughed. People began to drift back to the beer tent. Napoleon, who felt it was partly his fault that the first speech had been rained off, decided to help. What the audience needed was something exciting to look at. He dropped to ground level, and slithered over the damp grass towards the platform.

Lady Marchbank was looking particularly grim. By the time she was able to deliver her (rather witty) little speech, there would be no audience left. What a bore the Chairman of the District Council was – his speech was the same every year! But no, what was this? Lady Marchbank sat bolt upright in surprise. A ripple of laughter ran through what remained of the audience. The Chairman, who had just made a joke, felt his spirits rise. He could not see what the onlookers saw; a spiralling cloud of steam which was creeping along his shoulders like a ghostly boa constrictor. Everyone stared. The farmers came out of the beer tent to see what was going on. Wisps of steam began to emerge from the Chairman's ears and, with his shiny red face, he looked as though he was about to explode.

"And may I finish," he concluded, "by reminding you of the numerous sideshows we have for your entertainment – coconut shies, clay pigeon shooting and, of course, the wrestling bouts. An excellent opportunity for all of us to let off steam!"

There was a hissing noise and a spurt of steam belched from his top pocket. The crowd rocked with laughter, and the Chairman, beaming with pleasure, sat down. He was highly gratified; he had never made a better speech. Even when he had practised in front of the mirror in his bedroom, he had never imagined such success!

Mr Mullett was drawn back to the scene of the Grand Opening out of sheer curiosity. What was all the laughter about? He was still angry with Napoleon and his temper was not improved when he found himself sandwiched between Mrs Mossop, the blatherskite (so called because she was such a gossip) and her very fat

neighbour, Mrs Tallentire. Mrs Tallentire started telling him all about her Johnny who was playing tenor horn in the band this year. Mrs Mossop started telling him about the extraordinary goings-on on the platform.

"They do say, Mr Mullett," she said grimly, folding her arms over her scrawny bosom, "that you've been getting ower friendly with some sort of clood. Not that I'm one to listen to gossip, of course, but it does occur to me that this bit of steam that's been making trouble oop there might have summat to do wid you!"

Mr Mullett looked towards the platform and blinked. Lady Marchbank had risen graciously to her feet to declare the Fair open. She had hardly begun to speak when a wall of fog rose from ground level and began to engulf the platform party inch by inch. Napoleon, it seemed, had become a little light-headed after his brilliant performance during the Chairman's speech and was now enjoying showing off.

The blatherskite set her lips in a thin line.

"See what I mean?" she said, looking at Mr Mullett through narrowed eyes. Mr Mullett groaned and clenched his teeth on his pipe.

Very soon, all that could be seen of the platform party was Lady Marchbank's head, adorned with a magnificent ostrich feather hat. The head seemed to be talking and the plumes nodded up and down as it spoke, but no one could hear a word. The public address system had chosen that moment to go on the blink – through no fault of Napoleon's – and all anyone could hear was what sounded like a pop concert from outer space. The whole effect was rather

ghostly, but the crowd loved it. So much better, they told each other, than all those boring speeches. The Chairman of the District Council listened to the roars of approval, and sat, content inside his own little fog, blissfully unaware that his audience had quite disappeared from view. And Lady Marchbank, who never noticed persons lower than herself anyway, was most pleased with the response to her speech. As for Napoleon, he was having the time of his life!

The only person who was not happy was Mr Mullett. With some struggle he managed to extricate himself from between the two fat ladies and made his way, grim-faced, towards the fog-bound platform. He was within ten feet of it when the 'fog' suddenly disappeared, leaving the crowd in unexpected sunshine. Napoleon was nowhere to be seen – unless you counted the innocent little white cloud which was floating upwards into the blue sky. Mr Mullett set his teeth round his pipe and rehearsed in his mind the few words he intended to say to Napoleon when he caught up with him. This time the cloud had gone too far! He would have to go!

Seeing Mr Mullett, Napoleon's heart sank. He had a strong suspicion he was in for more trouble, and as he drifted high above the busy fairground, he began to wonder again if being on a year's trial meant you could be sent back at any time. He hoped not, because he didn't think Mr Zeus would be too pleased to see him. He knew he had been showing off, and showing off had been the very reason Mr Zeus had decided to bring him down to Earth and give him to the Mulletts. Showing off, Napoleon remembered with

a sigh, had been the cause of all that nasty business in the Scilly Isles. No, he decided, he definitely did not want to be sent back to Mr Zeus in disgrace. He must think of some way of pleasing Mr Mullett; he must find good deeds to do to make him forget how angry he had been.

More cheerful now that his mind was made up, Napoleon hovered high above the big marquee. From there he could see everything that was going on. On the very edges of the Fair the gannan-folk were gathered, colourful groups of gypsies from all across the North Country who were busily engaged in buying and selling their beloved 'coloured' horses. The fastest of the fell runners were just scattering up the fell on the first steep slope of the race. In the main ring three little girls on fat ponies were fighting out the finals of the Junior Show Jumping. By the Gardening Society's tent five men were labouring over a long line of stones in a field – 'steean-wallers' who were competing against each other to see who could build the best stone wall in one day. A crowd had gathered round the poor perspiring entrants, all offering unwanted advice and criticism and sometimes laughing unkindly when one of the walls collapsed in a heap of rubble. Napoleon's heart went out to the steean wallers struggling with their heavy stones in the heat. He determined to give them some shade and was just drifting that way when he saw Mr Mullett standing right by the competitors, pointing with his pipe and offering comments to his neighbour. Perhaps not, he thought, and hastily floated up into the sky once more.

Just then, his attention was caught by a flash of silver and faint melodious notes drifting up to him on the breeze. Napoleon

changed direction and went down to investigate. The visitors to the Fair were being entertained by the Carrowbridge and District Brass Band. They had been playing for over an hour when Napoleon found them and they looked extremely hot – perspiration was streaming off their faces and every once in a while they got out their white handkerchiefs and mopped their scarlet cheeks. Napoleon felt almost as sorry for them as he had for the steean wallers. He arranged himself over the band in order to cast a pleasant shadow beneath.

Unfortunately, in his enthusiasm he got a little too close, and before he knew what was happening, he suddenly found himself being tossed about in the air like a matchstick in a raging torrent. At one moment there would be a terrible blast on the cornet and the cloud would be flung helplessly into the sky; at the next he would be sucked down and down as little Johnny Tallentire on the tenor horn once again forgot to blow instead of suck. It was not until Johnny's mum had leaned her large form over the euphonium (causing it to make the most peculiar noises) and clipped her Johnny on the ear that Napoleon suddenly found himself released – just in time to be shot skywards again as Mr Atkinson from Emblethwaite began his solo on the trombone. At one stage the cloud narrowly escaped being cut to pieces on the accordion, at which Ted Walker from the Post Office was sawing away on the edge of the group.

The air grew damper and damper. The instruments began to wheeze and cough in a most peculiar way, becoming harder and harder to play. Several people forgot to blow and Napoleon

half-vanished up the tube of the euphonium before Mr Mullett's friend Percy Hodgson remembered himself in time and blew out. Then Johnny Tallentire got the hiccups and not even another clip round the ear from his mum could get him back on course again.

Mr Mullett, standing in the stock ring a few yards away, heard the weird noises coming from the band and glanced over. In horror he dropped the halter he had been holding and Dawston Lad, his prize tup - never a well-behaved ram at the best of times – seized his opportunity and galloped over to the wire fence where he could scratch his horns in peace. It took Mr Mullett and two of the judges 10 minutes to disentangle Dawston Lad's long, curly, black horns from the fence and Mr Mullett was lucky not to be disqualified.

Napoleon had a vague sort of feeling that he was not making himself as popular as he had hoped and, badly in need of a few words of love and reassurance, went in search of Mrs Mullett. He had last seen her going back into the Women's Institute tent, where the judging for the best cakes, scones and desserts was about to begin. Napoleon sneaked into the marquee over the heads of the crowd.

The ladies had worked very hard. Cakes like wonderful palaces of pink and white icing rose above the snowy tablecloths. Mountainous meringues climbed towards the roof of the tent in their lakes of scarlet jelly. Napoleon looked around. The third trifle from the right temporarily distracted his attention from finding Mrs Mullett. He was almost sure it was hers – it looked just like the one she had loaded so carefully into the Land Rover. He considered it critically; it was quite a good trifle, he decided, but not quite

tall enough. What it needed was another foot or two of meringue. And who better to provide a snowy-white, sparkling meringue than Napoleon himself?

The judges stopped in amazement in front of the enormous meringue, which towered five times as high as any other in the tent. Mrs Mullett gave a gasp of horror as she recognised Napoleon.

"This has to be the winner!" exclaimed the Chairman of the District Council, who was one of the judges. A smirk of pride hovered on the lips of Lady Marchbank, whose trifle it was.

The Chairman reached behind him to where his assistant was holding a tray of labels announcing First, Second, Third and Highly Commended. He lifted out the bright red flag for First Prize. Lady Marchbank's smile grew broader.

The red flag was attached to a sharp plastic stick. The Chairman reached up and stuck the flag in the very top of the magnificent meringue. The meringue gave a small scream and rose sharply into the air. Lady Marchbank's mouth fell open in surprise. The rest of the trifle and what was left of the real meringue collapsed with a damp plop.

"Oh," said Lady Marchbank, pink with embarrassment.

"Well, really!" said the judges.

"Cheat!" muttered someone in the crowd, just loud enough to be heard by all the onlookers. Lady Marchbank went bright red and stalked out of the tent. Napoleon sailed out behind her with a slight list to starboard, looking a little sheepish. He tried to catch Mrs Mullett's eye to ask forgiveness, but Mrs Mullett was looking steadfastly at the trampled grass of the tent floor, wishing that she

could dig herself a hole and hide from the world for a couple of days. Napoleon winced as he heard her whispering fiercely to herself: "Mr Mullett was right! There's nowt else for it. That clood will have to ga!"

It is never pleasant to be jabbed in the starboard quarter by a sharp plastic stick when one is minding one's own business being a peace-loving meringue. That, and the angry words from the normally gentle Mrs Mullett, left Napoleon feeling sore and unwanted. He drifted off again in search of love and attention elsewhere.

Lady Marchbank was in a very bad temper after the business of the trifle. She was judging the last class of the afternoon in a few minutes and decided to sit down in the Very Important Persons tent for a while with a soothing cup of tea. On her way there she suddenly stopped, rooted to the spot. Wafting in front of her was the top half of her trifle!

"You!" she said in an icy voice and Napoleon's insides turned to snow. "What are you? And what were you doing on top of my trifle?"

"He's a pet of Mr Mullett's!" said someone in the crowd and everyone giggled. Thanks to Mrs Mossop, the story of Mr Mullett and his 'clood' had spread all round the fairground.

"A pet!" snorted Lady Marchbank. "What sort of animal is it?"

"Folk say it's a cloud!" shouted someone else and the crowd roared with laughter.

"Well, whatever it is, it should be kept under control!" declared Lady Marchbank, quelling the laughter with a look. "Where is this

. . . this Mullett person?"

Napoleon groaned inwardly. Someone consulted his programme.

"He should be in the ring now, for the Champion Bull Class. Right good bull he had there – sure to win."

"Oh, really," said Lady Marchbank, sarcastically. "Perhaps I might be allowed to make up my own mind about who is likely to win? After all, I am the judge!" And she strode off purposefully. Napoleon followed at a safe distance. Mr Mullett might need his help!

Lady Marchbank was looking forward to judging the Champion Bull Class. She reckoned she knew a thing or two about livestock because her father, Lord Canoven, had bred a champion herd of Aberdeen Angus and as a little girl she had been allowed to scratch their noses. Of course, she hadn't had much to do with them since, but she still thought cows were rather sweet. Besides, it would be pleasant to say a few well-chosen words to this Mr Mullett. And if he thought he was going to win with his beastly little bull after what had happened to her trifle, he was going to be very disappointed!

But there was nothing sweet or little about Mr Mullett's Fresian bull. His eye had an evil glint to it and he was by far and away the biggest and strongest bull in the whole of Carrowbridge district. Once, when Mr Mullett's cowman Fred had been leading the bull along by a long pole attached to a ring in his nose, the bull had turned around and gently dusted the cowman along the drystone wall with his horns. Fred had been in hospital for a week and afterwards applied for a job as a shepherd. Even Mr Mullett, who had reared Merrowlay Mountain Meadow from a spindly little

calf, would no more have turned his back on his prize bull than jump off a crag with his hands tied behind his back. Lady Marchbank, however, had no such fear. She was convinced that she had a way with animals – all animals, even bulls.

But no one really has a way with bulls. Even the kindest can have an off day, and Merrowlay Mountain Meadow was not a kind bull. Furthermore, he was definitely having an off day. Mr Mullett was feeling extremely nervous. This was the most important class in the show for him and he did not want anything to go wrong. Right now, he felt he was attached to almost a ton of seething, simmering bad temper; it was like being handcuffed to a large time bomb with a very short fuse.

Lady Marchbank, tactfully assisted by an expert from the Ministry of Agriculture, had got almost to the end of the judging. The bulls were behaving beautifully and she fancied she was doing rather well. Merrowlay Mountain Meadow was announced over the loudspeaker and Lady Marchbank, leaning over the Ministry man's shoulder, saw Mr Mullett's name beside the bull's. She smiled as she thought of what she was going to say to him.

Merrowlay Mountain Meadow had a very hot head. His nose was dry and he was tormented by flies which landed on his ears and buzzed in a tight circle just out of reach. He hated the flies, he hated Mr Mullett and most of all he hated the horrible, brightly- coloured waving thing which his short-sighted little eyes could dimly see at the other side of the ring. He hated it with all his heart and he wanted to squash it flat.

It was Lady Marchbank's hat. Lady Marchbank, unaware of the

waves of hatred coming at her from the bull, was still occupied with thinking how she was going to squash Mr Mullett. She had her back to the ring. Suddenly a gasp of consternation swept through the audience. With a cold feeling she could not explain, she swung round. Across the ring, a massive bull was pawing at the ground and staring straight at her with a very unpleasant look in its eyes.

Lady Marchbank may not have known a great deal about livestock but she knew enough to recognise that she was about to be charged by a very angry bull, which stood between her and the only exit; and as she stood rooted to the spot, digesting this interesting fact, the animal thundered straight at her, bellowing furiously. Mr Mullett was tossed aside like an autumn leaf in a gale. The crowd stood stunned and silent, waiting for the awful impact. Nothing like this had ever happened before in the entire history of Carrowbridge Fair.

But then, suddenly, when the bull was halfway across the ring, a strange and wonderful thing happened. An impenetrable fog settled in front of the bull's eyes so that he could not see an inch (or even a centimetre) in front of his face. But the fog did not make him angrier, as well it might. It was so quiet in there. Someone was singing a song close by which made Merrowlay Mountain Meadow remember all sorts of lovely things – how he liked to gallop on the high pasture with the wind in his nose; how crunchy and sharp the first spring grass tasted when he was let out of his pen after the winter; how he used to lie in the cool shade of the great oak when he was a tiny calf. All at once the irritations of the long hot day fell away from him like an old itchy skin, and before the eyes of the astonished onlookers he laid his massive head on the grass of the

ring and the great bulk of his body collapsed gently behind him.

Within seconds he was fast asleep.

There was a round of spontaneous applause from the crowd and a babble of excited voices. Mr Mullett, still a little shocked, picked himself up and hurried towards the huge bull which slept so peacefully in the middle of the ring. But he had no time to feel grateful to Napoleon because at that very moment the cloud was whisked away by a playful breeze and the bull, woken from his pleasant dreams, opened his eyes and got to his feet. Once more Lady Marchbank found herself rooted to the spot as Merrowlay Mountain Meadow, with Mr Mullett running helplessly alongside, moved towards her at a steady trot. There was another gasp from the crowd.

The bull stopped beside Lady Marchbank. She stared in horror at the huge horns and the ring in the nose only inches from her face. Then the bull opened his mouth and a long pink tongue shot out and sloshed Lady Marchbank on the cheek.

It was rather like being hit hard with a length of wet sandpaper.

A look of complete astonishment passed over Lady Marchbank's face and the spectators held their breath, wondering what she would do next. To their astonishment, she smiled broadly and leant forward to pat the bull on his neck. What a sweet little bull he was! She had always known she had a way with animals, and now, all by herself, she had tamed a furious bull!

Well, it was true that she had had some help from that irritating little cloud. but still . . .

She shook hands warmly with Mr Mullett and, amid loud

applause, pinned a giant red rosette on Merrowlay Mountain Meadow's halter. Mr Mullett beamed, lifted his cap to Lady Marchbank and decided that maybe she wasn't such a bad old stick after all. Napoleon, hovering out of sight at the edge of the crowd, breathed a sigh of relief.

The animals were loaded into the truck, Jed drove off in high good humour because Bess had won the Sheepdog Trials, and Dawston Lad was shut securely in the back of the Land Rover. Napoleon was floating about over Mr Mullett's head, hoping for a lift, but not daring to say anything in case he was still in disgrace. All around them tents were being struck, trucks and trailers were reversing in and out of gateways, the jumps were being dismantled in the show ring and there was a delicious smell of rabbit stew coming from the caravans of the gannan-folk. Mr Mullett turned at last to Napoleon.

"Well, mi lad," said Mr Mullett severely. "I have to tell thee that there were times today when I decided you'd definitely got to ga, year's trial or not!"

Napoleon shrank miserably into his centre, hoping he wouldn't make a fool of himself by having an emotional outburst.

"We'd just about had enough of thee today," continued Mr Mullett, "what wid the carry on wid the speeches and the trifle and as for the noises thoo got to come out of that band . . . that wus a miracle!"

Napoleon dared to look at Mr Mullett's face. Far, far down inside Mr Mullett's hard blue eyes, he thought there was the slightest suspicion of a twinkle. But Napoleon cast his eyes down

once more and tried to look sensibly ashamed.

"But I don't mind saying – seeing as I'm a fair man – you saved my bacon this afternoon, with calming the old bull down and all. I don't know how you did it, but he's been a different beast ever since. Went into the truck as gentle as a lamb."

Mr Mullett drew deeply on his pipe.

"Aye, I'm a fair man," he repeated. "And I've no doubt you meant well all along. Thoo's such a great gowk for turning folks on their heads!" Mr Mullett shook his head disbelievingly.

"I never saw owt like that bull of mine . . . noo shift thee backside into t'van and we'll git garn!"

On the way home, jammed in with the empty cake tins, Dawston Lad breathing lovingly down her neck, and Napoleon slolloping damply about on her knee, Mrs Mullett still managed to do some knitting and sing quietly to herself. Despite the trifle, she had won two prizes for her scones, one for her jam, and the cup for her early vegetables. Every once in a while, she gave a little giggle.

Mr Mullett looked at her sharply as they bumped up the fell track.

"Have you been at Atkinson's parsnip wine agin, lass?" he enquired with that same twinkle in his eyes. "By Gaw, it packs a punch or two!"

The previous year Mrs Mullett had been one of the judges in the home-made wine competition and it had had a marked effect on her on the homeward journey.

Mrs Mullett shook her head and giggled again.

"It was just what you said, Mr Mullett," she told him, "about

Napoleon saving our bacon, I was just thinking – he didn't only save your bacon. He saved your beef as well, the great gowk!"

And they laughed all the way home.

A breath of sea air

Afterwards, everyone agreed with Mr Mullett that it had been a gay fine day, and for several weeks Napoleon wafted along in high favour. The farm was slowly ripening in the full summer. The hay had been brought in. Napoleon had played an invaluable part by keeping the skies clear until the big baler (which Mr Mullett had hired at vast expense from his miserly neighbour, Mr Sourworthy) had scattered a neat trail of bales across the two hay fields.

The goslings had outgrown their yellow and black fluff and a peculiar combination of feather stuck out of them at all angles while Nature decided what to do with them. The barley was a swatch of gold in the bottom valley, which moved with a pattern of wind and cloud; Napoleon spent hours creating swirls and shadows on its surface when he had nothing better to do - which wasn't often in this busy time. At last, when the weather was so vital to all the growing things, he found he was really needed. It was a shame that occasionally his enthusiasm ran away with him, as when the "patch of shade" which Mr Mullett had requested became an uncontrolled downpour, turning the top field into a quagmire and marooning the tractor for two days up to its hub caps in mud.

Mrs Mullett had other things than the farm on her mind. All through the dark winter days she would look forward to her own special day in the year. And now, as the occasion of the annual Women's Institute outing to Silcombe Bay approached, she took

time off from feeding the pigs and collecting the eggs to slip up to her bedroom and take down from the top of the wardrobe the heavily-boned swimsuit which Mr Mullett had bought her on a distant trip to the sea when they were young. But it was the same every year. With a regretful shake of her head she folded it once more in its tissue paper wrappings and buried it under the old copies of *Farmers Weekly*.

"No," she told herself firmly. "It wouldn't be seemly. Nowt but mutton dressed as lamb!"

And she would tiptoe downstairs again and out into the dusty sunlight in the yard, as though ashamed of awaking old memories.

Mr Mullett, although allowed on the trip as a 'dependant,' was not at all keen. He objected strongly to being called a dependant, and protested, with monotonous regularity, about giving up a valuable day when the barley harvest was almost upon him. In fact, every year, as the day grew nearer, Mr Mullett grew more and more difficult.

"You know you love Silcombe," Mrs Mullett said persuasively, as they sat in the kitchen one warm summer evening. "And every year you're glad you took a day off from the farm to enjoy yourself!"

Mr Mullett looked gloomy.

"Well, I don't know," he said at last. "What about the beasts? Who's going to take care of them, I'd like to know? And we're harvesting barley the day after tomorrow, if t' weather holds. I don't think I can take time off from the farm after all!"

Mrs Mullett sighed in exasperation.

"Jed can look after the beasts," she said firmly. "And the barley'll still be standing whether you go or not!"

"Aye, that's as mebbe," conceded Mr Mullett unwillingly. "But what about the blatherskyte? You know I can't abide that woman! If she sits near me on t'coach and starts clattin' her silly head off, I 'll git off at t' first stop and walk home!"

"Mrs Mossop may not even be going this year," said Mrs Mullett soothingly. "And even if she is, there's no need for you to have owt to do with her."

"That woman puts me in a fair temper," said Mr Mullett heatedly. "She could talk a banty cock into laying an egg!"

"Aye, she's a terrible body to clat," Mrs Mullett agreed. "And since Napoleon came to us she's had plenty to talk about!"

"Well, if I'm garn wid you," said Mr Mullett forcefully, "Napoleon will have to stay here. I'm not having owt said about cloods to spoil my day - the spiteful owd acid drop!"

Napoleon, who had been listening to the conversation from his favourite spot on top of the kitchen table, was about to protest, but Mrs Mullett looked at him and shook her head. It would be no use trying to move Mr Mullett. Even Mrs Mullett said that persuading him to do something he didn't want to do was harder than pushing Carrock Fell over with a matchstick. And now she had got him to agree to going to Silcombe for the day, she did not want him upset again.

Napoleon floated moodily out of the door and up the fell. The beck bubbled thinly below him. The day's heat, stored in the ground, came blasting up at him. It was very hot and parched - how lovely it would be to spend the day at the seaside! Napoleon had been keeping himself dry so as not to spoil the harvest. But how

joyful it would be to soak up gallons and gallons of splashy sea water and have a good rain out over the sea, where it couldn't do any harm. He swooped down and hovered over the duck pond. The ducks and their half-grown ducklings were squabbling over a few inches of muddy water - all that was left of the pond. Napoleon knew how they felt. Oh, for the misty, moisty, rainy feeling of the sea . . .

It would not have surprised anyone who knew Napoleon to have seen, a few days later, a small white cloud sailing over the coach as it bowled down the main road on its way to Silcombe. Napoleon was determined not to make a nuisance of himself this time. He was determined not to get in the way. He certainly did not want Mr Mullett to see him. But nothing, absolutely nothing, was going to keep him away from the wind and spray of Silcombe Bay.

Mr Mullett was feeling very put out. By the time the coach had arrived at the bottom of the fell track to pick up Mr and Mrs Mullett, it was almost full and the only two seats left were smack in front of the blatherskyte. Mrs Mullett had a lot of trouble stopping Mr Mullett from getting off the coach there and then.

"Not brought that clood of yours with you then?" Mrs Mossop started as soon as they settled in their seats. "Because we're hoping for a lovely sunny day and we don't want no clarty owd cloods spoiling our sunbathing!"

Mrs Mullett tried to smile. Mr Mullett gave the blatherskyte a look that would have been enough to stop a rooster in full crow. But it had no effect whatsoever on the blatherskyte. She poked her whiskery face in between the seats and settled down for a lengthy

gossip. Before they were halfway down the Silcombe road, the Mulletts had learned all about the current goings-on in Carrowdale. Had they heard that Mr Atkinson down at Emblethwaite got record prices for his lambs at the fat stock sale on Tuesday? Everybody knew Atkinson fattened them up till they were all blubber and slather and not fit for eating - it was a disgrace!

This last was too much for Mr Mullett. Atkinson of Emblethwaite was a good friend of his and a good farmer to boot. Mr Mullett rose majestically in his seat, removed his pipe from his mouth and pointed it at the blatherskyte.

"If thoo can't shut thee gob," he said slowly and clearly, "I'll put thee head in mi bucket!"

He raised the orange bucket in which he always packed his sandwiches and a bottle of beer, and shook it threateningly at Mrs Mossop.

Mrs Mullett buried her head in her magazine. The blatherskyte looked at Mr Mullett rather in the way a black widow spider sizes up her next victim. A lesser man than Mr Mullett would have crawled under the seat in terror but Mr Mullett's steady blue eyes looked straight back at her. The blatherskyte gave him one last venomous look and departed to the back of the bus, where she spent the rest of the journey telling anyone who would listen (and there were not many) how that dreadful Mullett creature used a wicked cloud machine to rain on his neighbour's crops.

At last the coach drew up in the car park at Silcombe Bay. No one noticed the small white cloud which hovered at a discreet distance from the coach and followed the Mullets as they

made their way down to the promenade.

"You shouldn't have been so rude to Mrs Mossop," said Mrs Mullett reprovingly when they were out of earshot of the coach.

Mr Mullett shook his head.

"I know that, lass," he agreed. "Thing is, I can take anything she cares to say about me without losing my temper. But when she starts on other folks, spreading her poison, then I can't stand it no more!"

Mrs Mullett patted his arm.

"Well, we're here now, and it's a lovely day. Let's enjoy ourselves and not fret about it."

It certainly was a lovely day. The waves slip-slapped happily on the beach, the sun sparkled on the blue sea and a fresh breeze kept everywhere deliciously cool. Mr and Mrs Mullett hired two deck-chairs from the man by the pier steps and took them down to a sheltered corner by one of the breakwaters. Mr Mullett took off his jacket and hung it carefully on the back of his chair. Then he removed his tie and rolled up his sleeves. Finally, with great daring, he undid the top button of his shirt. Then, with a deep sigh of contentment, he leaned back in his chair and closed his eyes.

"You're right, lass!" he said after a few moments. "It does a body good to get away for a holiday once in a while." And he fell asleep.

Mrs Mullett smiled to herself, took off her cardigan, put on a pair of sunglasses and got on with her knitting.

Napoleon was having a wonderful time. Far out to sea he swirled and swooped, playing footsie with the waves and taking in vast quantities of cold sea water. To him its bubble and zing were like the best champagne. He became quite heady with delight and

patted the crests with his trailing edges, giggling and singing to himself as he went. A passing gull, on its way to Silcombe Sands, curled its beak contemptuously as it made its way steadily across the sky.

"No time for playing in my day," it shrieked at Napoleon, looking down its beak disapprovingly at the frivolous little cloud cavorting below it. Napoleon stuck out a tongue and carried on with his games.

From where he floated Napoleon could see the tiny pin-sized figures which were Mr and Mrs Mullett sitting solidly in their deck-chairs. As the day wore on, Mr Mullett took out a clean white handkerchief, knotted it at the corners and placed it on his head to protect him from the fierceness of the sun's rays; then he went back to sleep. Mrs Mullett decorously removed her stockings under cover of a towel and tiptoed down to the sea for a quick paddle in the amber shallows. Later on, they had lunch out of the orange bucket which Mr Mullett referred to as a 'bait box.' Mrs Mullett privately wished that Mr Mullett would have a little more regard for appearances and buy a picnic basket; she was a bit ashamed of the bait box, although she knew she shouldn't be.

Later still, as the shadow of the pier began to lengthen across the sands, Mr and Mrs Mullett made themselves respectable once more, packed up the plastic bucket and went for a stroll. Napoleon, who was still dreamily floating above the waves, glanced over and saw them disappearing up the steps to the prom. He panicked and, forgetting that he had absorbed an awful lot of sea water, raced inland, riding on the onshore breeze.

The Mulletts were nowhere to be seen. Napoleon flew the whole length of the promenade, screwing himself into a tight ball with anxiety. It was rather like squeezing a waterlogged sponge. He had just arrived over the head of the blatherskyte, who was sunning herself on the far end of the prom, when it happened . . . he felt himself coming down with a heavy shower. Cold rain cascaded over Mrs Mossop, who leapt to her feet and covered her head with a copy of *The Cumberland News*. Within seconds it would have made excellent papier mache.

Napoleon tried to move himself away, but in vain. He seemed to be stuck in a mini-depression. The blatherskyte looked up from under her sodden newspaper and recognised him.

"You!" she screamed, and there followed a list of extremely unpleasant things she would do to Napoleon if she ever caught up with him.

By now a little crowd of people had collected. They were very interested in the spectacle of the deck-chair thunderstorm. Where they were standing, ten feet or so away, the sun shone down and melted their ice creams; but there, in the eye of the storm, a short fat cloud was raining cats and dogs on a short fat woman underneath, who in turn was screaming with rage.

"Perhaps it's the circus come!" said a small boy hopefully. "Perhaps she's a clown!"

At last a kindly thermal whisked Napoleon away, leaving Mrs Mossop almost speechless with anger, especially when several members of the crowd threw money into her upturned sunhat to show their appreciation.

Napoleon, deeply ashamed, made his way back towards the pier. He wondered what he would do if he could not find Mr and Mrs Mullett. He couldn't remember the way back to the farm. Even the prospect of the terrible telling off he was likely to get, when Mr Mullett heard about the blatherskyte and realised that Napoleon was at the seaside when he was supposed to be at home, was better than never getting back home at all.

He was just floating unhappily through the turnstile on the pier (without paying) when he caught sight of one of the coach party going into a tent which was decorated with moons and stars. It was Mrs Mullett's friend, little Miss Turnbull, from the Carrowbridge Sweet Emporium. If he stuck with her, sooner or later she must meet up with the Mulletts! He hovered over the tent and peered down the small opening in the top.

Miss Turnbull was having her fortune told. She was sitting opposite Madame Zara, the clairvoyant, who was gazing into a crystal ball. Miss Turnbull was twisting her hands uneasily in her lap; she had a very important question to ask the clairvoyant.

"What strange event do you wish me to foretell?" The clairvoyant asked in a gloomy voice. She was exotically dressed in a long scarlet robe and had something over her head which looked remarkably like a table runner with bobbles on. Miss Turnbull stared at her and swallowed nervously.

"My young man," whispered Miss Turnbull at last. "The one I have brought with me on this outing today - he's rather shy and I want to know . . . I want to know if he's ever going to ask me to marry him!"

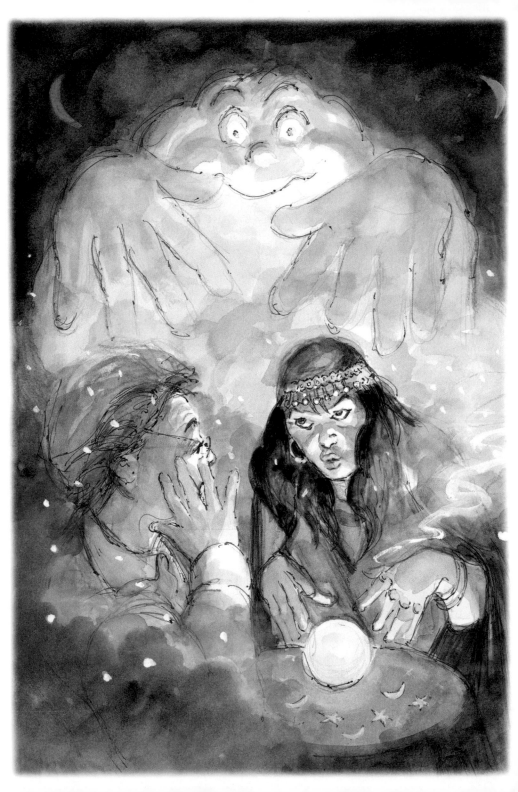

She finished in a rush. Miss Turnbull had been walking out with Horace Ponsonby for 15 years and the whole of Carrowbridge was waiting for him to pop the question.

Madame Zara passed her hands once or twice over the crystal ball.

"I see a tall, dark man," she muttered, looking at Miss Turnbull out of the corner of her eye. Miss Turnbull looked puzzled.

"I see a short dark man," she tried hopefully. Miss Turnbull considered for a moment and then shook her head regretfully.

"I see a short, fat, balding man," said Madame Zara irritably. A beatific smile spread over Miss Turnbull's plain little face. For a moment she looked quite beautiful.

"That's him! Bless his heart!" she said wistfully.

Madame Zara leaned forward to look into the crystal ball once more - when, with a brilliant flash, it exploded! Or so it seemed, for suddenly the tent was filled with multicoloured smoke which spun and twirled. Flashes of rainbow light beamed out from the table. Sparkling rain fell from the roof. Silent lightning flickered from wall to wall. Napoleon was showing off again. Miss Turnbull ran screaming from the tent, leaving Madame Zara, her table runner slightly askew, looking wonderingly into her crystal ball, which had finally reappeared in the swirling smoke.

"I knew I had the Power," she said in an awed whisper, clasping her hands together. "I shall be famous now!"

Mrs Turnbull, however, who had never been so frightened in her life, ran straight into the comfortably round shape of Horace Ponsonby, and clinging to him for dear life, sobbed hysterically

about thunder and lightning and fireworks. Horace found the embrace of Miss Turnbull rather pleasant and by the time he had quietened her down enough to take tea with him in the pier kiosk, he found himself asking her to be his wife.

Napoleon had intended not to frighten little Miss Turnbull but merely to give her better value for her money. Madame Zara's performance had struck him as wishy-washy in the extreme, especially as it had cost half a crown to cross Madame Zara's palm with silver. So he was rather upset to see Miss Turnbull dash screaming out of the tent. But fortunately, making a hasty departure himself through the same hole in the roof he had used to come in, he chanced to look around and see Miss Turnbull, her head resting blissfully on the shoulder of Horace Ponsonby. Napoleon had not had much to do with people in love, unless you counted Mr and Mrs Mullett, but even he could see that though Miss Turnbull might be sobbing her heart out, she was very happy indeed. How strange human beings were!

But where were the Mulletts? He could not see them anywhere. He was just thinking of going up the promenade once more to look for them when the most extraordinary sight met his eyes - tame clouds, pink and blue and green, being carried around on sticks. Napoleon stared in disbelief. It could not possibly be true. A strong breeze was blowing across the pier, whipping up spray from the high tide, but these clouds never moved, except when their keepers waved them about on the end of their arms in an excited manner. And then came the worst shock of all - the people, mostly children, who were holding the tame clouds, were eating them . . . actually

taking great mouthfuls of them and swallowing them! Napoleon felt he had strayed into some awful nightmare. Pink, blue and green clouds, imprisoned on wooden sticks, being eaten by their owners. It was too terrible. As he shuddered with horror a few drops of rain fell on the holidaymakers below, causing them to scurry for shelter.

He pulled himself together, steeling himself against the lively wind which threatened to whip him away from the pier. He felt as though he were witnessing some ghastly cannibal rite. He had a sudden moment of panic. What if he were to find himself caught on one of the sticks? What frightful fate might befall him? It was unthinkable.

Then Napoleon noticed that all the people with coloured clouds on sticks were coming from the same wooden building, close to a huge wheel, about halfway down the pier. He braced himself for action and took advantage of a favourable gust to float over and investigate. A sinister humming noise was coming from within. Keeping close to the roof, he wisped inside.

He could hardly suppress a gasp of fear. What horrifying tribal ceremony was this? Here before him, a high priestess, elaborately dressed in shocking pink overall and multicoloured earrings, a snowy white cap covering her hair, was bending over a large metal bowl. As the bowl spun, the high priestess poured strangely coloured crystals into its centre, muttering to herself the while; and then she took a stick from a nearby jar and wound it, with slow elaborate ceremony, around the silver sides. There in the spinning bowl there suddenly appeared a shimmering web of silken strands, which she caught up on the sticks into fragrant clouds of pink and blue and green.

Napoleon was reminded of the great cloudmakers in the sky and, drawn by an irresistible fascination, he went nearer. The high priestess continued her incantations.

"Can't you make oop your mind yet, lad? There's pink ones and green ones and blue ones. Surely you can choose one or t'other."

Napoleon found himself looking straight down at a smudgy-faced boy who was so small he could hardly see over the counter. He was gazing at the high priestess with his finger in his mouth.

"I want a yaller candy floss!" said the little boy.

At once, everything clicked into place. Napoleon gurgled with relief and amusement at his foolishness. The crowd in the hut looked about, perplexed, as the sudden, unmistakable sound of water being let out of a bath filled the air. But all that was to be seen was a slight mistiness against the roof. Candy floss! thought Napoleon. How silly of me! Of course he knew all about candy floss - Mrs Mullett had said you could buy all sorts of goodies at the seaside - ice creams and toffee apples and candy floss. So that was what it was!

"I've told you already," the lady in the shocking pink overall said crossly. "We don't have any yellow ones. Just blue ones and pink ones and green ones. That's always been enough for most folk!"

Napoleon felt sorry for the little boy. He slipped out of the kiosk and, as the wind caught him, swirled high into the sky above the pier until he was looking down at the brightly-coloured, strolling crowd below him. He looked this way and that, trying hard to think of an idea. Yellow candy floss? How was he going to do it?

On the other side of the pier, in the shelter of the pavilion wall,

a man was selling paper cups of orange and lemonade. He did not seem to be doing very well; there was, after all, a chilly evening breeze now and not many people were hot and sticky enough to fancy a cold drink. Nevertheless, he had lined up several cups of lemon and several cups of orange on a table in front of him, hoping to tempt the passers-by, so he was rather annoyed when a persistent little cloud came and hovered just over his stall, cutting out all the sunlight. He was even more annoyed, as well as utterly astonished, to watch the lemonade suddenly twirl up from his paper cups like water spouts in a hurricane. People stopped to watch. It was by far the most original sideshow they had seen so far, better even than the dolphins. The lemonade spouts grew higher and higher and thinner and thinner; little sucking noises came from the paper cups like several dozen naughty boys drinking through straws in a bad-mannered way. Finally the spouts vanished into the small white cloud above, which was slowly turning a fetching shade of citron yellow.

The crowd applauded and shouted for more until they were hoarse. Napoleon (who had slightly overdone it) treated them to a light shower of lemonade and then hitched a lift on a passing gust in the direction of the candy floss kiosk. Meanwhile the crowd, rather dry after all that cheering, was queuing up at the soft drinks stall. The salesman shrewdly put his prices up.

Napoleon slipped back into the dark interior of the little hut. He floated over to the spinning bowl and rained, in a gently drizzle-ish way, over the crystal strands.

"Ooooh!" said the candy floss lady, licking the back of her hand.

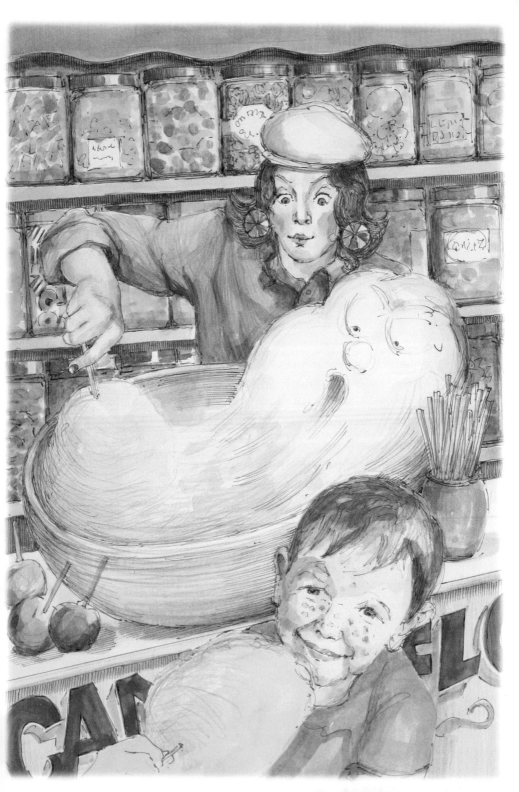

"That tastes nice!"

"Ooooh!" shouted the smudgy-faced little boy as he peered over the counter. "You're a genyus, miss! You done a yellar one!" He took an enormous bite out of his yellow candy floss. His eyes widened.

"An'," he gasped stickily, "an' it tastes of lemonade!"

But for Napoleon tragedy had struck. In floating down to the level of the revolving bowl, he had caught one of his edges among the sticky tendrils of sugar which glittered like a dewy web and now held him trapped as surely as a butterfly in a spider's larder. He struggled and struggled, but slowly and surely he found a huge chunk of himself being drawn into the bowl. He was wound around with sticky threads like a cocoon and finally whipped up onto a stick and offered to the next customer, who - horror of horrors - turned out to be none other than the blatherskyte herself!

Napoleon was whisked out of the kiosk, still attached to those bits of him which were parcelled up in the candy floss, and forced to float helplessly behind the blatherskyte as she strode off down the pier. She was making, Napoleon realised unhappily, for the far end of the pier where Mr and Mrs Mullett were leaning on the rail, looking over the side and enjoying the invigorating air.

Mrs Mossop had in mind a few well-chosen words which she had been rehearsing with relish - mostly about eccentric old farmers who kept ill-controlled clouds as pets, but with a few other spiteful remarks thrown in for good measure. Napoleon struggled desperately as they drew closer to the Mulletts. He was trailing unseen behind Mrs Mossop, but once Mr Mullett turned round he could not fail to see his cloud hanging helplessly in the sky over the

blatherskyte's head. Napoleon gave one final heave that wrenched the candy floss from Mrs Mossop's hand, and sailed skywards on a gusty breeze.

Mrs Mossop whirled round just in time to see her candy floss rocketing off into space on the end of a familiar-looking cloud.

"You!" she screeched. "Just you wait . . !"

But Napoleon was not waiting. He took off as fast as he could and did not stop until he was just short of the stratosphere, where he was very nearly changed into cirro-cumulus. So when Mrs Mossop stormed up to Mr and Mrs Mullett with a cock and bull story about "that dratted clood" stealing her candy floss, as well as soaking her into the bargain, there was a cloudless blue sky as far as the eye could see. Mrs Mullett kindly suggested that perhaps Mrs Mossop might have been sitting too long in the sun. Mrs Mossop turned the colour of a ripe tomato and stormed off.

Tempers cooled as the time approached for the high spot of the outing - the traditional ham tea at the very best of Silcombe's old and respectable tea rooms, Hepplethwaite & Macey's, which had been laying on ham teas since Queen Victoria was on the throne. Mr and Mrs Mullett made their sedate way down the prom towards the imposing, white-painted facade of the tea rooms.

Napoleon, who had been suffering from the scorn and derision of a flock of badly-brought-up seagulls, very nearly missed them again. The gulls seemed to find the sight of Napoleon trailing the remains of a candy floss screamingly funny, and made lightning raids on the sticky strands of sugar until they finally came unstuck and fell into the sea. The cloud only caught up with the Mulletts

as they were entering the revolving doors of Hepplethwaite & Macey's.

Napoleon had a little trouble with the revolving doors and by the time he finally arrived in the dining room, with its cane chairs, white tablecloths and flock wallpaper, he was breathless and a bit tattered. If the head waiter had caught sight of him, he would undoubtedly have been asked to leave for lowering the tone of the establishment. But the head waiter had not had any instructions about clouds; and anyway all he noticed was a slight mistiness around the chandeliers.

Tea passed uneventfully. Napoleon kept well away from the meringue which arrived with the second course and by lurking furtively behind a pillar he avoided the sharp eyes of both Mr Mullett and the blatherskyte, who were sitting at opposite ends of the long table and did not even have to ask each other to pass the sugar.

It had been a long and happy day. On each side of the table were ranged the shiny sunburned faces of the Carrowbridge farmers, shopkeepers and craftsmen and their wives, with a sprinkling of the younger generation. They had lost all their shyness and there was much laughter and reminiscence. Even the blatherskyte was cheerful now. She had discovered that their waitress was her sister Lil's niece (by marriage), and was busy catching up on the more scandalous side of Mossop family life.

At long last, after belts had surreptitiously been loosened several holes, and grandfather's gold watches ponderously removed from a dozen pockets and scrutinised through a haze of

well-being, the party decided it was time to go. They collected their holdalls and carrier bags, full of sticks of rock for nephews and nieces, put their hats on at the door and eventually set off along the prom towards the car park where they had arranged to meet the coach. Nobody noticed in the final scramble that Mrs Mossop had been left behind. She was still deep in conversation with her sister Lil's niece (by marriage) and missed the departure of the other W.I. members and their dependants. In fact, so deep in conversation was she that even when the vacuum cleaner whirred round her feet and the number two waitress came to clear the table, Mrs Mossop sat glued to her seat. Who would have thought the saga of the Mossop family could be so enthralling?

At last Lil's niece (by marriage) made a regretful departure to catch her bus. The tea rooms were by now deserted. Mrs Mossop hastily gathered up her bags as she suddenly realised she had been left behind. She bustled into the Ladies to powder her nose, shutting the door behind her. Seconds later, the floor manager locked the revolving doors, and turned the key firmly in the lock of the Ladies with no idea, of course, that anyone was still inside.

Following Mr and Mrs Mullett back to the coach, Napoleon kept an uneasy eye open for Mrs Mossop. There was no sign of her, but he still kept a safe distance. He did not want to spoil things now by being spotted at the last moment, especially as he was rather hoping to sneak into the back of the coach and hitch a lift home.

There was a strong offshore breeze now and he would be battling against it all the way home - an unnatural way for a cloud to behave at the best of times. Several bottles of beer were being taken

aboard and he was sure that in the sing-song and generally jollity a little extra mistiness would hardly be noticed.

All went exactly according to plan. Napoleon managed to slip up the steps of the coach, effectively camouflaged by the giant panda which Mrs Tallentire, senior, was taking home for her grandson, and which she had won in the Pier Bingo. The cloud looked round carefully as he tucked himself tidily on top of the luggage rack. It was all very well dodging the odd flying mackintosh, but what about the blatherskyte? There was an empty seat just below him. What if she came and sat in it? It would not be long before she rumbled him and told Mr Mullett. But there was still no sign of her.

Everyone was feeling very jolly and already three husbands on the back row were singing a (rude) version of D'ye ken John Peel, much to their wives' disapproval. The President of the Women's Institute stood up, stooping slightly against the roof, and scanned her list in a casual fashion.

"Is everybody here?" she asked, peering through the smoky dimness of the inside of the coach."

"Yes!" everyone roared back good-naturedly. No one noticed that the blatherskyte was missing. Then, with his extraordinary earsight, Napoleon suddenly heard her. She was calling for help! There wasn't a moment to lose.

The driver clambered into his seat, looked in his mirror and started the engine. As the coach began to move away from the car park, Napoleon poured through the wide meshes of the luggage rack and twined himself around Mr Mullett's neck, at the same

time letting out one of his ear-splitting shrieks, guaranteed to galvanise even the sleepiest old nag into a Grand National winner in three seconds flat. Mr Mullett shot ceilingwards, cracking his head forcibly on the small sharp notice that said 'Please Mind Your Head While Leaving Your Seat.' Mrs Mullett dropped the orange bucket with a clatter, scattering her knitting and the remains of their lunch, while several W.I. members fell off their seats into the narrow aisle. The bus driver, convinced that his engine had blown up, jammed on his brakes and put his head between his knees.

"Thoo gormless great gowk!" Mr Mullett shouted, as soon as he had recovered enough to recognise the cloud. "I might ha' guessed thoo was behind it . . . why aren't yer back at t'farm where thoo belongs?"

There was a babble of voices, all angry with Napoleon for causing such an upset, and it was several minutes before he was able to explain about Mrs Mossop. She was, he told them a little smugly, locked in the Ladies at Hepplethwaite & Macey's.

Mr Mullett eyed the cloud suspiciously, but as there was no doubting that the blatherskyte was not aboard the coach, he and the President of the Carrowbridge and District Women's Institute set out for the tea rooms. Even if Napoleon was not telling the truth, it seemed a sensible place to start the search. Fortunately, the floor manager who had locked up that evening, lived only two doors down the road. So, in a matter of minutes, Mrs Mossop was released. The floor manager, very apologetic, offered her a free meal the next time she visited Silcombe "to make amends, dear lady, for any distress caused." And as a final gesture he removed

the pink carnation from his buttonhole and pressed it into her hand. Mrs Mossop was quite unused to such attention. The late Mr Mossop had been a man of few words who spent most of his life on the sofa asleep under a copy of *The Sporting Times*. She was speechless with amazement and hardly spoke a word during the whole of the return journey.

"Miracles," said Mr Mullett, pulling his cap down over his eyes, "will never cease!" And he promptly fell sleep.

Mr Sourworthy gets his comeuppance

For the next few days Napoleon thought it would probably be wise to keep out of Mr Mullett's way. Mrs Mossop did seem to have turned over a new leaf, which was surely in Napoleon's favour; but the rescuing of the blatherskyte, though praiseworthy, was not in itself quite enough to wipe out the lingering annoyance Mr Mullett felt at the fact that Napoleon should have disobeyed him and gone to Silcombe after all.

The cloud was aware of this, and secretly regretted that he couldn't have rescued someone just a little bit more popular than the person Mr Mullett loathed with every fibre of his being.

But soon all such trivialities were forgotten in the need to harvest the barley before the weather broke. Mr Mullett walked ceremoniously into the field one morning and rolled an ear of barley in his hand.

"She's ready!" he said at last, and looked up at Napoleon. "Can yer keep watch, lad? If thee friends come near tell them to hoof it, will yer?"

Napoleon was delighted to be able once more to show how useful he could be. He buzzed around all day while the combine churned lazily below, and right up to dusk, when the sky was smoky with barley dust dancing in the evening light, he kept any vagrant clouds at bay.

It was a splendid harvest. Mr Mullett had worked very hard indeed, and there was no doubt that Napoleon's weathering had helped a great deal. The last trailer load was taken to the barn. Mr Mullett returned the combine to his neighbour, who received it with ill-grace, despite the fact that Mr Mullett had paid handsomely for the loan. The cloud and Mr Mullett walked happily back to the farm kitchen, for once in total harmony.

But in the heart of Mr Sourworthy there was only black envy. He had seen the golden barley flowing in abundance out of Mr Mullett's field. He probably knew better than Mr Mullett how many sacks the harvest would yield, for Mr Sourworthy made it his business to know everything about Mr Mullett, who did so much better than he did in every respect. Mr Mullett's beasts always won prizes at the shows, year after year; Mr Mullett's harvests (although sometimes poor) were always better than Mr Sourworthy's.

He couldn't understand it. Didn't he spend a small fortune on sprays and machines, while old Mullett had nowt but a tractor? Mr Sourworthy could not bring himself to admit that Mr Mullett worked very hard on his farm while he, Mr Sourworthy, was very lazy indeed. Mr Sourworthy was sure that Mr Mullett had some secret machine which helped him on the farm. He would have liked to get one for himself so that he could do even less work. But how was he to find out what it was?

The very next day the answer came to him. He was sitting in the Baker's Arms, alone as usual, brooding over the price Mr Mullett's bullocks were fetching at market, when Mrs Mossop settled herself

down at the next table with a glass of port and began sounding off to her companion about that "clood" of Mr Mullett's. Mrs Mossop's change of heart had not lasted long.

"If you ask me," she said confidentially, loud enough for the whole of the snug to hear, "he uses it as some sort of weather machine! It's a wonderful thing, mind! Can hear any sort o' sound 50 mile away, I'm telling you! And you jest push some sort of switch to get rain or hail or snow! I've seen it with my own eyes. Wonderful it is. Rescued me from the jaws of death back at Silcombe!"

Mrs Mossop - the blatherskyte - was in full swing once more, making mountains out of molehills.

Mr Sourworthy supped the last of his pint in a daze. He was sure now that his years of suspicion about Mr Mullett had been right. No wonder his neighbour's harvests were so much better than his own. What he, Mr Sourworthy, could do with a machine like that! The sky, quite literally, was the limit. Mr Sourworthy decided to spy on Mr Mullett secretly and find out all he could about this wonderful weather machine.

The very next day he climbed up the fell and loitered on the edge of Mr Mullett's land, pretending to look for stray sheep. Soon he caught sight of Mr Mullett, walking up the fellside with Old Tom at his heels. Directly over his head hung a fluffy white cloud which swooped up and down as the currents caught it. Every once in a while, Mr Mullett would look up, point his pipe at the cloud, and issue what sounded like a list of instructions. In actual fact, Mr Mullett was scolding Napoleon for making his ghost noises in the hen house and putting the hens off laying; but to

Mr Sourworthy's tortured mind it was the final proof he had been looking for.

"So it's true!" he said to himself. And there and then he determined to get hold of this weather machine and keep it for himself.

During the next few days Mr Sourworthy was often to be found up on the fell, pretending to look for stray sheep but actually spying on Mr Mullett and his cloud. He began to notice that when Mr Mullett was not about, the sheepdog Tom and the cloud were usually together. In fact it was one of Napoleon's jobs to look out for 'cragfast' sheep up on the fell, where perhaps even Old Tom could not see them, stuck as they might be against the granite edge of the crag.

This gave Mr Sourworthy an idea and soon he had worked out a crafty plan to get hold of Napoleon and at the same time get even with Mr Mullett.

It was almost the time of the shepherd's meet, when the sheep were brought down from the fell, and those which had strayed from other farms could be returned to their owners. Each farmer's flock was easily recognisable by lig marks on the ear and the smit mark of the farm. The work of the collie dogs was very important in bringing the sheep off the fell; without the dogs, the farmer's job would be impossible.

Mr Sourworthy's plan was to steal Old Tom. Even with Jed and Bess to help him, it would still leave Mr Mullett in a rare old fix when it came to the shepherd's meet. And if he was very clever he would be able to lure the cloud away as well.

Soon his opportunity came. Napoleon and Old Tom were

crossing and re-crossing the fell; they were looking for a half-grown lamb which had become separated from its mother. Suddenly Old Tom heard a faint cry and Napoleon spotted a white shape under a rowan tree. The lamb was not hurt, just a bit confused, so it took only a few seconds to round it up and put it back with its mother where she grazed on the steep slope of the fell. They were so absorbed in what they were doing, neither of them noticed the Land Rover crawling up the fell track towards them, until the grazing sheep scattered in all directions.

Old Tom set up a frenzied barking. Mr Sourworthy advanced towards him, wearing a thick pair of leather gloves and before Old Tom knew what was happening, Mr Sourworthy had grabbed him. Within seconds he was tied up, helpless, in the back of the Land Rover.

Napoleon, who had been some distance away during all this, just caught a glimpse of Old Tom's tail as he was bundled roughly into the Land Rover. He had never liked Mr Sourworthy and he guessed at once what was going on, but unfortunately at that moment an unkind thermal swept him skywards, and by the time he had battled his way down to ground level the Land Rover was driving away at top speed. It was all Napoleon could do to catch up with it, even with the help of a strong following wind, but when he did at last manage to overtake, he hurled himself with a loud splat across the windscreen.

There was an instant, impenetrable fog. The Land Rover swerved and almost came off the track. Then the cloud remembered that Old Tom was inside and, with a noise like one of those toy arrows being

pulled off the bathroom wall, he hastily unstuck himself from the windscreen. It was a painful experience. He screeched and shot up into the sky, his extremities tingling unpleasantly.

Down the mile and a half of track which led to Mr Sourworthy's destination, the farmer found himself alternately rained on, sleeted on, hailed on and snowed on – all to no avail. Mr Sourworthy just chuckled to himself. His plan was working perfectly! He shuddered to a halt outside an old dilapidated barn which straddled the side of the fell. There were no other buildings nearby and it was miles from any road. It suited Mr Sourworthy's purpose admirably. Within seconds he had opened the back of the Land Rover and dragged the snarling, protesting dog into the barn. Napoleon shot in after him, still raining and snowing and fogging all over Mr Sourworthy as hard as he could. It did not make a scrap of difference.

Mr Sourworthy tied Old Tom to the far wall with a piece of rope. Then he looked up and saw the cloud hanging menacingly above him. He smiled.

"How about coming to wuk for me?" he asked.

Napoleon's reply was a stinging shower of hail.

"Now steady on," said Mr Sourworthy, brushing himself down hastily. "If you want your precious master to have his dog back, I should think again if I were you. I can get a good price for a fully-trained sheepdog somewhere where off-comers don't know him. Why should I bother to give him back? But if you were to work for me, now, that would be a different matter. I could do with summat to control my weather, such as that cheating Mullett has

had all these years. You think about it. You work for me and I'll give back the mangy old cur – no questions asked. It's shepherds' meet tomorra and I'd hate to see our Mr Mullett without his dog. I'll be back at sunrise tomorra. So I can either let the dog go, or, if you won't see sense, tek him away and you'll nivver see him again."

And before Napoleon could recover himself, Mr Sourworthy had whipped out of the door of the barn with a surprising turn of speed for one so fat, slammed it in Napoleon's face and turned the key. They were trapped!

When the autumn dusk began to fall and Old Tom still had not returned for his food, there having been no sign of either him or Napoleon all day, the Mulletts began to grow anxious. Before the last of the evening light failed, they hastily finished off their tasks and set off up the fell. Mr Mullett went one way and Mrs Mullett the other.

"Tom boy! Tom boy!" called Mr Mullett, giving his own particular chirruping whistle, but there was no answering 'woof' from the empty fell. Mrs Mullett scanned the sky, hoping that Napoleon at least would return and help them in their search, but the only clouds to be seen were the black fingers of approaching night.

Jed and Bess came up to join them and all night long they walked the rolling fell which sailed like a ship through the starry dark. Once Mr Mullett heard a distant barking from high up on the beckside, but as they moved towards it, they heard the cry of a vixen returning the call.

"It's nobbut the young fox on his first outing," said Jed. "Time he was mekking off on his own, I reckon." And as they listened, a chorus of yapping barks echoed through the night, faded into the distance and was gone.

Just before dawn they trudged wearily down the fell path to the farmhouse. In an hour it would be time to rouse themselves and get ready for the shepherds' meet.

"Caught in a trap, mebbe," said Mr Mullett gloomily as he pulled off his boots. "And where the heck is Napoleon? There's summat fishy garn on here."

And both he and Jed fell into an exhausted sleep, while Mrs Mullett kept a vigil by the window, anxiously hoping to catch a glimpse of Old Tom and Napoleon returning.

Mr Sourworthy could be very clever when he wanted his own way. He seemed to have thought of everything. All night long, while Old Tom dozed uneasily at the end of his rope, Napoleon prowled round the old stone barn, looking for a way out. Even a tiny chink would have been enough. But Mr Sourworthy had carefully blocked off every hole with bundles of old rags. There was no escape. Then Napoleon had an idea. He swooped down over Old Tom and did his special shriek in the dog's ear. Tom leapt up as though he had been stung, his old yellow fangs snapping at air. Napoleon retreated hastily.

"What did you have to do that for?" snarled Old Tom bad-temperedly.

"Sorry!" said Napoleon humbly. "I didn't know how else to wake you up and it's rather important. We haven't got much time."

The barn was totally dark. The single window had been boarded up. But Napoleon felt deep in his insides that sunrise was approaching.

"Listen!" he said urgently. "I've got a plan to get us out of here and teach old Sourworthy a lesson he won't forget. Are you game?" The collie danced on the end of his rope, panting enthusiastically.

"You bet!" he woofed. "What do we have to do?"

The collie spent the next ten minutes gnawing at his rope, urged on by Napoleon. When it was three quarters bitten through he hurled himself forward with all his might. After the third attempt,

the rope parted suddenly and Old Tom shot across the barn into a pile of straw.

"What now?" he snuffed, pawing barley awns out of his ear.

"Hurl yourself against the door, just by the lock!" said Napoleon.

"Awful lot of hurling in this job!" the dog complained, but he set to with a will. Napoleon positioned himself over the door, listening with his supersonic ear-sight. If only, if only . . . yes, the key had been left in the door, they were in luck. Several hurls later, Napoleon caught the faint sound of something metallic falling to the ground outside.

"You can stop hurling now Tom. It's my turn to go to work," Napoleon said.

The collie collapsed thankfully onto the floor.

Napoleon wound himself round and round like a fleece being spun into yarn. Faster and faster he twisted and twizzled until Old Tom was too dizzy to watch him. He grew thinner and thinner and longer and longer. Finally, when he was as thin as a strand of wool and so long that he stretched at least three times round the barn, he began to feed himself through the keyhole.

"Wait here!" he said to Old Tom rather unnecessarily, as the last few centimetres of him slithered through the lock. "I'm off to find the wind."

There wasn't much time left. Already the hills were lit from behind by the rosy flush of the approaching sunrise. Any minute now Mr Sourworthy might arrive and all would be lost.

Napoleon spiralled upwards through the dawn. Higher and

higher he rose above the fell, until he felt the first tremor of the morning wind. He whistled loudly. The wind grew stronger. He whistled again and a miniature tornado suddenly seized him and twisted him about in a mad dance.

"Stop! Stop!" cried Napoleon. "I need your help. We must be quick! Oh, do stop it and listen!"

Napoleon had laid his plans only just in time, for there on the brow of the hill, where the first red light of morning flooded the bracken with colour, appeared the fat figure of Mr Sourworthy.

Mr Sourworthy was in a bad temper. He did not like having to get up at dawn on a cold morning. He unbarred the door and reached for the key to unlock it.

"Blast it!" he muttered to himself, as he was forced to bend double over his considerable stomach and grope about in the dust.

"I'm sure I left the key in the lock yesterday. Must have fallen out in the night, I suppose."

And he fitted the key back into the lock and undid the door. He opened and shut the door very quickly as he squeezed his large bulk inside.

"Mustn't give that pesky cloud a chance to escape!" he panted, as he leaned on the door to get his breath back. And perhaps it was the sound of his own breath in his ears which prevented him from hearing the soft sigh of wind and cloud as they sneaked in behind him, just in time.

It was totally dark in the barn. Mr Sourworthy fished a torch out of his pocket and shone it round. The dog was no longer tied to the wall. Eventually Mr Sourworthy spotted him, lying with his head

between his paws, growling softly and menacingly. There was no sign of the cloud. Mr Sourworthy shone his torch around the rafters.

"I know you're up there somewhere, cloud!" he sneered. "You'd better give me your answer now, or this dog is going to find himself sold this morning at Cloughdale market!"

There was complete silence. Even Tom had stopped growling.

Mr Sourworthy advanced cautiously on Old Tom and made a grab for him. The dog would have dearly loved to take a chunk out of Mr Sourworthy, but a faint, familiar voice from somewhere high above told him: "Lie still! We want him to open the barn door."

Mr Sourworthy was pleasantly surprised when Old Tom allowed him to tie another, rougher rope around his neck and lead him towards the door. He opened it a crack. Suddenly, without warning, he found himself in the grip of a hurricane. The straw in the barn whirled round and round as the wind howled and the dust blew up into his eyes. He lost his grip on Old Tom, who did not need any further invitation and shot off like a rocket up the side of the fell towards home and his master.

But the wind had not finished with Mr Sourworthy. He was picked off his feet and blown straight out through the barn door. Higher and higher the hurricane twirled him into the sky, spinning him over and over, until he forgot which was up and which was down. And sometimes he found himself in the middle of a thick white fog which giggled at him and confused him even further.

"Stop!" he shouted. "Please stop! If it's you doing this, Mr Mullett, I really don't want your weather machine – you can

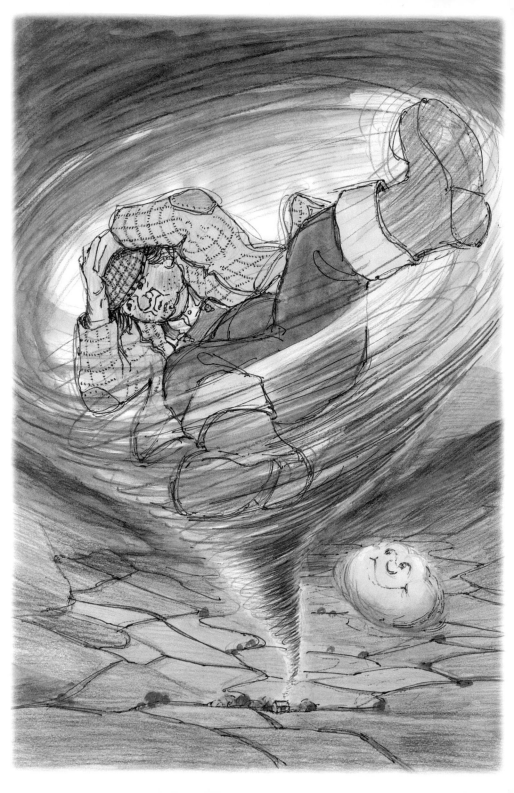

keep it! Help . . . !" And he found himself once more swooped up into the sky as though he were no more than a dead leaf. Up and up, high above the fell, until it was so cold that an icicle formed on the end of his nose. Then, just as suddenly, he found himself hurtling at a terrifying speed towards the ground.

"I'm sorry I've been so ba-a-a-d!" he shrieked, quickly remembering to say his prayers. "I won't do it again! H-E-L-P!"

He closed his eyes in despair, then a moment later opened them as, suddenly but quite gently, he came to land. Feeling a bit dizzy, he looked around to see where he had landed, and discovered he was sitting on the very edge of a precipice. Mr Sourworthy groaned. There was no way up or down. He was well and truly stuck.

Meanwhile Mr Mullett was scanning the fell as he leaned on his shepherd's crook. The sheep were dotted all across the fell, as though a giant hand had taken a handful of tiny white pebbles and scattered them willy-nilly up and down the crags. Jed was already up there, working the lower sheep into the intake fields. In an hour or two it would be time to meet up with his other neighbours and exchange the stray sheep. But how in tarnation was he to get all his flocks down without Old Tom to help? Bess was a good dog, but no one could work sheep like Old Tom. He did not even need telling.

Well, it was no use standing here moaning. There was work to be done. With a sigh, Mr Mullett started off up the fell – a strangely lonely figure without his familiar dog at heel. Suddenly a black and white bullet streaked across the fell towards him. It hurled itself at his legs in a frenzy of delight, and Mr Mullett ran a rough and loving hand over the old dog, his eyes misty.

"Someone's had thoo tied up," he said at last, as his fingers encountered a raw patch around the dog's neck. Tom licked him ecstatically. "By heaven, I'll have the devil that's done this to you!"

And he set off up the fell with Old Tom at his heels to begin work bringing the rest of the sheep down into the valley. Already the lanes leading to Fairfeld, the ancient hill where the meet had taken place for generations, were jammed with flocks coming down to Carrowdale, and more farmers were coming over the hill. There was no time to waste – Mr Mullett didn't intend to be shown up by anybody.

It was nearly dusk before Mrs Sourworthy got really worried about her husband and telephoned the Mountain Rescue. A team of searchers arrived at the farm just as darkness washed up to the brow of the hill, and they set out at once with dogs and powerful torches. It did not take them long to locate Mr Sourworthy, perched on a sharp crag and feeling very cold and very sorry for himself. They had a hard time getting up to him, but at last they managed to parcel him up on the end of a rope and lower him to safety. It was an uncomfortably bumpy journey and he had to endure a great many humiliating jokes about how so rotund a person could possibly have scaled the most difficult peak in the mountain climbers' manual, but Mr Sourworthy said nothing.

He had had a lot of time to think, stuck up there all day, and he had decided he could not possibly tell anyone what had happened to him. Most of it no one would believe anyway, and the rest . . . well, Mr Sourworthy was rather ashamed of the rest.

"It's funny," remarked Mr Mullett to his wife over breakfast the next morning. "Old Sourworthy getting stuck up on that crag just as Tom comes galloping home."

He looked thoughtfully at Napoleon, who blushed a pretty pink.

"And where was our Napoleon all the time, I'd like to know?"

But Napoleon had hastily floated out of the window and up over the farm. He thought it would be wise to avoid having to answer any awkward questions. Mr Mullett watched him go and shook his head.

"If that airy-fairy piece of nonsense has been oop to his tricks again," he said, stabbing his fork into a fat pork sausage, "he'll have to go!"

"Yes, dear," said Mrs Mullett. "But I think we should find out what really happened first, don't you?"

So for the next few days nothing more was said. In fact, Mrs Mullett was beginning to think they would never know what the true story was when, quite unexpectedly, a round, fat figure appeared at their farm gate. It was Mr Sourworthy. Mr Mullett eyed him suspiciously as he crossed the yard. Every few seconds his neighbour glanced nervously up at the sky, as though he expected to be pounced upon from a great height.

"I've come to offer you the free loan of my combine, or any of my machines," said Mr Sourworthy with a cringing smile. Mr Mullett's pipe almost dropped out of his mouth in astonishment.

"After all," Mr Sourworthy continued with a ghastly grin, "we neighbours must help each other . . . and not bear grudges!"

A gust of wind caught at his cap and blew it off.

He gave a squeak of terror.

"You haven't . . . you haven't got your weather machine out today?" he asked in a trembling voice. "Because I've come to tell you that I shan't be bothering you any more. Me and Mrs Sourworthy will be moving soon – I'm starting up in the second-hand car business. But in the meantime . . . " (he gave another yelp as the playful autumn wind whipped at his trouser legs) "I did want to tell you that I would be delighted to help you in any way I can."

Mr Sourworthy looked up and noticed the cloud hovering over his head.

"That business about the dog," he said hastily. "Just a little misunderstanding." The cloud darkened visibly and there was a rumble of thunder. "I won't stop to explain . . . " Mr Sourworthy gabbled as he sprinted out of the gate. "Regards to the wife!"

A short sharp snow shower caught him before he had gone ten yards.

"Napoleon!" said Mr Mullett in his sternest voice. The cloud, on the brink of pursuing Mr Sourworthy's stout figure down the fell path, hesitated and finally wavered his way back to Mr Mullett.

"I think you'd better tell me what all this is about," Mr Mullett said quietly. "What's this about Old Tom? And why is Mr Sourworthy frightened of my weather machine, as he calls it? I'm taking it he means you! What 'av yer been up to? Come on, lad, out wid it!"

So Napoleon had to tell the whole tale. Mr Mullett grew grimmer and grimmer as the cloud described how he and Old Tom

had been kidnapped and kept in the barn. But when Napoleon explained how he, Old Tom and the wind had given Mr Sourworthy his comeuppance and a free trip up the fell into the bargain, Mr Mullett's weather-dyed old face took on a most peculiar expression. He was trying very hard to look stern, but something was going awfully wrong with his features.

"Well, thank you, Napoleon," Mr Mullett said when the cloud had finished at last. "I'm right glad to see you both back safe and sound, but just remember, you mustn't use your power against folks that don't understand it. Now go on down to the house and I'll be there in two shakes."

And Napoleon, feeling rather deflated, floated slowly down the hill.

Mr Mullett waited until Napoleon was out of sight. Then his face creased in an enormous grin and he began to laugh.

"Ooh! I'd have given owt to be there!" he gasped. "Old Sourworthy whisked up into the air by that pair of rapscallions!"

And he leaned against the drystone wall and laughed and laughed until his sides ached. Far, far above him, in the deep and endless blue, Mr Zeus, reclining on a thermal, laughed, too, so that thunder rolled across the sky and lightning flashed.

Meanwhile, back at his farmhouse, Mr Sourworthy, fearing the wrath of the dreaded weather machine, dived into the broom cupboard and shut the door very, very tight behind him.

The trouble with television

The harvest had been a bumper one. Rows and rows of fat barley sacks slumped against one another in the great barn. Good hay stood in three stacks around the yard. Strings of fat onions decorated the walls of the outhouse. The shelves of Mrs Mullett's larder glowed red and purple and green with jams and chutneys.

It had been a good year, and Napoleon, all in all, had played his part. Now the winter was drawing in – the time when the earth rested and curtains were drawn for the long evenings in the farmhouse kitchen. Birds were stripping the scarlet berries from the rowan tree. The autumn ploughing was done, ready for the frost to do its work. Winter was winging down from the north and Skiddaw would soon wear her first cap of snow.

But while the farming year took its normal course, there was still change at work on the fells. The year before, workmen had begun erecting a tall metal mast. Standing on top of one of the higher, grassy fells, it could be seen from anywhere in the valley. Mr Mullett called it 'a dratted nuisance,' and a number of farmers thought it was bound to upset the weather.

Napoleon had cruised up there occasionally, just to keep an eye on things. Once he had come upon a group of demonstrators with large placards. They were protesting about the mast being there at all – they said it interfered with the wild beauty of the fells.

The farmers didn't know anything about that, but they did know that the workmen had been dropping their plastic bags all over the heaf so that the sheep ate them (with dire consequences). So they joined in the protest as well.

But now the mast had started transmitting television pictures, a great deal of the opposition evaporated. Previously, the only kind of pictures anyone in the valley could receive were the kind which sliced people up and put them back together the wrong way round, or rolled them round and round the screen until it made you feel quite sick to look at them. Now, the farmers found they could watch football without losing sight of the ball altogether, and their wives were able to watch the travel programmes about sunbaked beaches without seeing them through a perpetual snowstorm.

The mast was hailed as an electronic miracle and people stopped grousing about it. Television suddenly became a popular pastime.

In fact, for a while, the television turned Carrowbridge life topsy-turvy. The Reverend David Hornsby-Smith found the reason for the falling Evensong attendance in *The Radio Times*; it was not that he was losing his touch – he just couldn't compete with television. The W.I. was badly affected, too. They had to rearrange their usually popular 'Flower Arranging Through the Seasons' series because of lack of interest. Some members even complained that the Wednesday night meetings clashed with the thriller serial.

Mr Mullett maintained his hearty disapproval of the whole business. And the night The Carrowbridge Arms installed a television in the bar and disrupted the dominoes tournament was a

black night indeed. He came home in a very bad temper and told Mrs Mullett in no uncertain terms that he would never have one of those contraptions in his house and that was that!

But the next day, Mr Mullett went to visit his old friend Percy Hodgson, and, as Fate would have it, Mr Hodgson's daughter had just bought him a television. When Mr Mullett came in the back door as usual, there was his old friend glued to the screen in rapt attention.

"Shhhh!" hissed Mr Hodgson, waving his hand at Mr Mullett in a rude and unsociable manner. Mr Mullett opened his mouth to protest, but then he caught sight of the screen and he was lost. For there before him was the one thing which Mr Mullett loved to see above all else – the sheepdog trials, live from Castlemere, and in colour!

Mr Mullett was very late home that evening, and when he came through the kitchen door, his eyes had a glazed look. Mrs Mullett was quite worried and fussed about him like a mother hen. But it was not until he was seated in his favourite chair by the fire, and had lit his pipe, that he came out with it.

"Mrs Mullett," he said solemnly, pointing at her with the stem of his pipe, "it's time we got ourselves yan o'them television sets!"

Mrs Mullett dropped her knitting with a start. The last time Mr Mullett had mentioned television he had sworn he would never have one in the house. And everybody knew how hard it was to change Mr Mullett's mind.

"Do you know," he went on after a pause, "I was sat in Percy Hodgson's front room and them dog trials were going on over at

Castlemere, near as you are to me! Dogs running oop t'fell, and Packisson – what farms far side of t'fell – he were there, looking as cross as sticks cos his owd dog didn't win. Aye, that was a good sight," he chuckled.

Napoleon, who was twined around the rocking chair, was intrigued by the conversation, and glided softly over the floor until he rested at Mr Mullett's feet.

Mr Mullett took a few puffs of his pipe.

"Do you remember," he continued, "the times me and Old Tom would go over the fells for t'trials? I would take a bit of bread and cheese in my pocket and we'd be all day getting there and back!"

He shook his head in amazement.

"And there I was, in Percy Hodgson's front room, seeing it all as clear as day!"

Mr Mullett had been a great man at the trials. He and Old Tom had once won every award for miles around and he missed the excitement.

For a few days Mr Mullett thought about what he had seen in Percy Hodgson's front room in his slow, thorough way. Napoleon, who had been fascinated by all the talk of this amazing machine, hung about him impatiently.

"Wouldn't do to rush into it," he said to Napoleon one morning, as he was mucking out the pigs. "But with the evenings drawing in, there's no doubt it would be company for Mrs Mullett when I'm out on the farm."

Napoleon was sitting on the half-door, more out than in (he was not too keen on the smell of pigs), and he grinned to himself.

He took a sly peep at Mr Mullett, who was standing lost in thought, a forkful of muck halfway to the barrow.

"And there are always the sheepdog trials . . . " put in Napoleon artfully.

"Oh aye," agreed the farmer absently; and then he gave a guilty start and grinned. "Aye, lad, we could give it a go, don't you think?"

Napoleon could hardly wait for the next day when Mr Mullett was due to go down to Carrowbridge Market. Mr Mullett was gone longer than usual and came back looking pleased with himself. He had made arrangements to hire a television from a local rental firm. Sure enough, the day after, the television rental van came crawling up the track to Home Farm, with Old Tom barking indignantly alongside.

The first few days were wonderful. Mrs Mullett discovered a series about a Yorkshire farm which she could criticise acidly all the way through and thoroughly enjoy at the same time. Mr Mullett and Percy Hodgson visited each other's houses to watch the local trials on Cumbrian television. They got so excited trying to tell the competitors what to do that Percy Hodgson spilt his glass of beer over Napoleon, causing him to giggle tipsily all evening. Napoleon was particularly fond of the travel programmes, but he so irritated the Mulletts by recounting his experiences in the Tropics, or insisting that he was a personal friend of one particular cumulus during a programme about Monsoons, that he was banned from watching them.

The farm began to wear a slightly neglected air. There had never been enough hours in the day to do everything before and now,

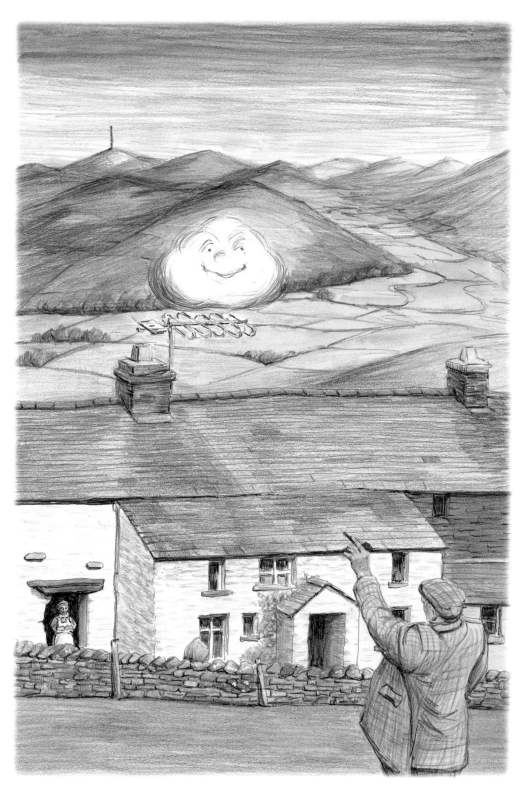

although the beasts were always well cared for, little things began to fall apart. A wheel came off the wheelbarrow while Mr Mullett was carting muck. He had been meaning to fix it for several days, and now there was muck all over the front path instead of on next season's potato patch. Mrs Mullett's washing line frayed and snapped and her whites ended up in the mud. Mr and Mrs Mullett almost fell out over that, as it had been several days since Mrs Mullett had asked her husband to fix it.

Then Mrs Mullett discovered the six o'clock news. It took her a week or two, because she had always brought the old horse in from his pasture at that time of the evening; but now that the winter chill was in the air he was tucked up warmly around four o'clock and by six Mrs Mullett would just be sitting down for her tea.

The six o'clock news had a bad effect on Mrs Mullett. On the first evening, when Mr Mullett came in from the evening milking, he found Mrs Mullett sobbing into her handkerchief.

"All those killings and fightings!" she wailed. "What is the world coming to . . ?"

After a few evenings of this, Mr Mullett put his foot down and banned the six o'clock news and the nine o'clock news as well, although by that time Mrs Mullett was usually dozing over her knitting. Mrs Mullett went back to reading *The Cumberland News*, which told her absolutely nothing about what was going on in the outside world but dealt with the really important things in life, such as fat stock prices in the markets and whether they were going to flood the valley beyond Mallow Fell.

One day, though, when Mr Mullett was late back from market

and Mrs Mullett was waiting for her rosehip jelly to set, she switched on the television for a few minutes, and once again, when Mr Mullett and Napoleon came into the kitchen, there was Mrs Mullett in tears. But this time she steadfastly refused to give up watching the news.

"What happens if the world blows up and we don't know a thing about it?" she said firmly.

So after that at six o'clock each evening, she would sit down in front of the television with her lips in a thin determined line and nothing and no one could budge her, even though by the end she would usually be crying bitterly into her hanky.

Mr Mullett and Napoleon were always out at that time – it was evening milking and time to bed the beasts down for the night. But one evening Mr Mullett paused in the act of hosing down the passageway in front of the cows and looked at the cloud, who was trying valiantly to be helpful without getting spattered in muck.

"Tha knows," said Mr Mullett in his broadest Cumbrian, which he always slipped into when he was feeling particularly serious about something. "I'm reet sick of this television nonsense. Noo will thoo look at Mrs Mullett. I've nay doot that it's a grand thing in its way . . . knowing aboot all them politicals. But it seems to me the world's so busy fighting with itsel' it's like having a pack of dogs quarrelling on yer doorstep. You can nivver get away from dratted worrying and barking. I tell yer, I don't like the world I see on that blasted contraption, not one bit ('cepting dog trials of course). That world's not for the likes of us. I've only jest gitten used to folks in this yan, and I'm too old auld for change, I reckon."

This was a very long speech indeed for Mr Mullett and he had been so absorbed in it that he had absent-mindedly directed the hose into the top of his Wellington boot, out of which water was soon overflowing into the passageway.

Napoleon nodded gloomily. What little he had seen of the television certainly had not lived up to his expectations at all. It looked unreal, somehow – more like the picture on the front of the jigsaw puzzles which Mrs Mullett had been so fond of doing before the television came. He remembered one in particular – cows grazing in front of an old-fashioned house, with a blazing blue sky above and one single cumulus cloud sailing well above the statutory levels laid down by Mr Zeus – and even Napoleon could see the cows were overdue for milking and there was not a cowpat in sight. Television seemed a bit like that.

Worse still was the effect it had had on Mrs Mullett – she was getting as snappy as an old ferret. Only yesterday she had thrown a saucepan at him when he had accidentally put out the fire she had just lit. It was not like her at all; something had to be done.

"Perhaps if I go and sit with Mrs Mullett at teatime . . ?" Napoleon suggested, as he followed Mr Mullett's squelching progress down the cowhouse and out of the door. "When she sits down to watch the news, I mean, I could stop her getting so upset – put a fog up, perhaps, when they show those awful bits which always make her cry."

"Aye," said Mr Mullett thoughtfully, as he emptied his Wellington boot into the dung channel. "That might work, you nivver know. Worth a try, any road."

So the next day Napoleon made sure he was drifting around the kitchen when Mrs Mullett sat down for her cup of tea. Sure enough, as six o'clock approached, she switched on the television and sat down in the armchair, cup of tea in one hand and hanky in the other. Napoleon watched her anxiously.

She was perfectly all right during the main item, which was the Queen's visit to the Scilly Isles (Napoleon winced as he remembered the Unpleasantness on the Cold Front) but as the news items and the pictures grew more upsetting she was soon crying hard. Napoleon was no better. He decided that the television world was perhaps not quite as cowpatless as he had thought. In fact, there were far too many cowpats. Instead of consoling Mrs Mullett, he felt a terrible rainy feeling coming over him and had to dash outside to have a quick cloudburst over the duck pond. When he got back, the news was over and Mrs Mullett was watching the football scores, looking very much happier.

Napoleon, however, suddenly found himself thrown into a turmoil. The newscaster announced: "Now for our weatherman, Egbert Duck, with the weather for today and tomorrow."

And there, bold as brass, was a man in a sports jacket picking up clouds and lining them up all over the map of Britain!

Napoleon rose out of his chair in horror. The weatherman smiled at the camera and proceeded to tell his audience that tomorrow would be sunny in parts (he leaned across the map and placed a few brightly coloured suns at intervals), with occasional showers in the East (here he shoved a big black raincloud, with a string of threatening raindrops attached to it, over East Anglia,

completely obliterating it) and snow (a giant snowflake wiped out the Shetlands) in the far North.

Gradually, Mrs Mullett became aware of a low humming noise. She turned in her chair. The noise was coming from Napoleon. He was turning a peculiar shade of purple, and as he did so he grew larger and larger and larger. All the time a noise like ten thousand angry bees was coming from his middle.

"Napoleon!" squeaked Mrs Mullett, thoroughly alarmed. "What is it? Whatever is the matter?"

A deep rumbling voice, not at all like Napoleon's usual happy one, came from somewhere within the cloud.

"That man!" roared Napoleon, trembling with rage in front of Egbert Duck, who was now happily drawing circles across the map to show everyone where the next Depression was coming from.

"That man is not Mr Zeus!"

"No, of course not, dear," said Mrs Mullett nervously, for she had never seen Napoleon angry before. "Why ever should he be?"

"Only Mr Zeus is allowed to move the clouds about!" bellowed Napoleon, his voice dislodging two pottery ducks, which fell into the fireplace

and shattered. "Only Mr Zeus arranges the snowfalls and the sun! Who is this imposter?"

And with that he shot over to the television and hovered angrily over it, trying to find a way in.

"Napoleon!" cried Mrs Mullett in horror. "It's only the weatherman. He just studies the weather and tells us what he thinks it's going to be like. He's only pretending to move the clouds about!"

But Napoleon wasn't listening. Egbert Duck had moved on to a satellite picture of the Earth and was pointing out a Cold Front which was likely to move over Ireland. The cloud fizzed with incoherent rage.

"He's . . . he's up in the stratosphere! With the Gods! This is too much!" And, finding a chink in the back of the television set, he started to feed his vast, purple puffiness into it.

"I shall find him! I shall find him! I'll teach him who's in charge!"

"No, no, Napoleon!" shrieked Mrs Mullett. "It's very dangerous. Don't touch that!"

But it was too late. There was a blinding flash. All the lights went out and the television screen went blank. Napoleon gave a loud scream, not unlike a kettle coming to the boil, and vanished in a cloud of steam.

Mr Mullett came bursting in from outside.

"What the heck . . ?" he shouted into the darkness.

"Help!" shouted Mrs Mullett. "Over here!"

Mr Mullett mended the fuses in grim silence and it was not until he was tightening the last screw on the last plug that, like an old

traction engine which has been building up a good head of steam and suddenly has to let rip on its whistle, he exploded with wrath.

"That," he said, flinging his cap towards the nail by the door and missing by a mile, "is that!"

Buttoning up his jacket with savage vigour and in a low-pitched rumble of rage, he added: "That's the very last time I let that – that puff o' nothin', that useless cuckoo spittle, muck oop my life! It's garn back where it come from! I'm nut having it any mair!"

And with that Mr Mullett wrenched the kitchen door open, picked his cap up off the cat, screwed it back on his head and slammed the door behind him . . .

Mr Zeus returns
with a flash

As chance would have it, the terrible bang from the television shot Napoleon straight up the chimney and he found himself sitting, bruised, sore and still very angry, on top of the aerial. Because he was a great deal cleverer than humans in several ways and had all sorts of extra senses, he knew immediately that all around him were strange signals called radio waves.

He knew that the spiky thing he was trying to sit on had come with the television and that the signals came to it, then, in some mysterious way, were converted into pictures on the television downstairs (when it was working). In a brilliant flash of inspiration he decided to follow the waves to their source and there he would undoubtedly find the horrible, the unmentionable imposter – Egbert Duck.

So that is exactly what he did.

He could both 'see' and 'hear' the waves and it did not take him long to home in on the transmitter on the hill. It was very disappointing. There was the tall transmitter, held up by its huge wires, with two red lights on the top to warn low flying aircraft of its presence. But nowhere, in the whole windswept space of the fell, was there any sign of Egbert Duck. There was a small building at the base of the transmitter and Napoleon had a good look in

through the window, but it was all locked up and deserted – not a trace of Egbert Duck anywhere.

Napoleon had risen up to the top of the transmitter and after a couple of tries had decided not to perch on the apex after all. He discovered that the signals did not stop at the transmitter but went on, away from the fell. He had just made up his mind to follow them when Hubert the Thunderhead came sailing majestically across the sky.

"Private Napoleon!" bellowed Hubert. "What are you up to now?" Napoleon winced, the condescending tone which the other clouds sometimes adopted was extremely painful to him. It was as though they expected him to be at the centre of a disaster. It was really too unfair. With as much dignity as he could muster he explained the serious business in which he was involved; he was sure that even Hubert the Thunderhead could not fail to be impressed. A human impersonating Mr Zeus! Moving the clouds about the sky! Altering the weather! It was surely not to be tolerated!

But when he had finished he was astonished to hear peals of thunderous laughter coming from deep within the dark cloud-caves of Hubert's insides.

"I do think you might take this more seriously," said Napoleon huffily. "After all, an imposter! It's a matter for the Olympic Committee! What would the other Gods say? They'd probably turn him into a spider! We must find him and stop him!"

Hubert the Thunderhead stopped laughing and explained slowly to Napoleon (with an occasional titter), that Mr Duck was just a weatherman, with a toy map of Britain, toy clouds, toy suns,

even toy snowflakes. He really did not do any harm. In fact he sometimes got the weather right, using scientific methods (that is, if the Olympic Committee was not using the cold fronts as squares on their three centuries old snakes and ladders game). Napoleon felt thoroughly deflated. He confided in Hubert that he had actually tried to get into the back of Mr Mullett's television set and had almost certainly ruined it.

Hubert sucked air in noisily through his non-existent teeth, causing a Force Ten gale over Kendal for approximately 15 seconds.

"I think you're in trouble there, old lad!" he said. "Mortals get very attached to their television sets – won't give them up after a while. I shouldn't go back there, if I were you. After all, they're only human. Ants on the face of the earth, I call them. No size to them, if you know what I mean. I wouldn't get mixed up with them if I were you."

Napoleon opened his mouth to protest loyally about Mr and Mrs Mullett and all the people he knew. Humans were certainly not ants. They were ants only if you were very high above them. Once you got close to the ground and saw their faces close to, they were all quite different. But he was too sore and tired and cold to argue. He wanted to find a cave somewhere and lick his wounds. He knew now that he could never go back to the Mulletts. After he had blown up their television and made an utter fool of himself? Never!

The following morning Mr Mullett went down into Carrowbridge and persuaded the engineer to come up immediately and take away the television. He said he would of course pay for the

damage, but no, he didn't want a replacement. He was finished with televisions once and for all.

The engineer looked puzzled.

"You'll miss it, mate," he counselled kindly. "Me missus would create something awful if she couldn't see her serial on a Wednesday."

Mr Mullett looked across at Mrs Mullett enquiringly. She shook her head.

"No thanks, lad," he said. "I've got a wheel on me wheelbarrow wants mending and a snaggy old beam in the cow byre and a couple of gutterings want fixing. I reckon I'll be too busy for that sort of carry-on."

"I'll be needing to finish that jigsaw of the Queen I started before we got the television," said Mrs Mullett. "And I've a thousand bits of baking to do. In fact, thinking about it, Mr Mullett, I don't know how we ever had time to have a television in the first place!"

But a little while later Mr Mullett went out into the back kitchen and found Mrs Mullett sobbing as she wrung an old cloth into a bucket.

"What's the matter, lass?" he asked kindly. "Is it the six o'clock news you'll be missing?"

Mrs Mullett shook her head and another tear trickled down her cheek into the bucket at her feet.

"No, that was just a bit of silliness. It's our Napoleon. Just look at this . . ."

And she tipped the bucket for Mr Mullett to see. Inside, there were a few inches of mucky water.

"Do you realise I'm mopping up our Napoleon? That's all that's left of our little cloud."

"What do you mean, lass?" asked Mr Mullett, not understanding at all.

"There was this great puddle of water behind the television," Mrs Mullett explained in a wobbly voice. "I've just finished wiping it up. And it's our Napoleon – he must have turned to water. There's nowt else left. But I can't bring missell to pour him down the drain. I don't know what to do!"

For a moment Mr Mullett stared hard at the water in the bucket. Then he sighed and shook his head.

"There, there, lass," he said, patting Mrs Mullett's arm kindly. "He's probably just lost some of his fluffs. Clouds can do that, you know. Not like folks . . . "

"Well, all the same, I'm not throwing him away," said Mrs Mullett firmly. "I'm that worried about him. He gave this scream, and then he just vanished. Where is he, I'd like to know, if he isn't in the bucket?"

All day Mrs Mullett walked about with red eyes and a handkerchief to her cheeks. By evening there was still no sign of Napoleon. Mr and Mrs Mullett went sadly to bed. Mr Mullett lay awake thinking about the harvest, and how Napoleon had helped him. He decided he had been rather hasty, after all.

The next morning Mrs Mullett was standing at the sink, washing up the breakfast dishes, when there was a slight sound behind her. She swung round. Mr Zeus was sitting at the kitchen table. He rose and doffed his hat courteously.

"Good morning, dear lady," he said in his singsong voice. "I just

drifted in to enquire about Napoleon. Behaving himself, is he?"

Mrs Mullett collapsed into the rocking chair and began to sob violently. Mr Zeus was a little embarrassed and, coughing tactfully, looked towards the window.

"He's vanished!" wailed Mrs Mullett. "Psst! Just like that. He won't come back! Not ever! And I was reet fond of him, and Mr Mullett was too, in his way – I reckon he's gay sorry he's gone, though he's that much pride he'd nivver admit it!"

"Dear lady!" exclaimed Mr Zeus, greatly distressed. "Pray do not give way to such showers and depressions. I am sure, if you will acquaint me with the whole sad story, I will be able to help you in a trice, if not before."

And patting her on the arm, he proffered a small, wispy handkerchief, which was no use whatsoever as it was composed entirely of cloud. Mrs Mullett took a deep breath, retrieved her own large white hanky from her apron pocket, mopped her eyes, blew her nose and began.

When she had finished her tale, Mrs Mullett took Mr Zeus through to the back kitchen to inspect the remains of Napoleon. Mr Zeus looked at the few inches of muddy water in the bucket and shook his head.

"No, no, dear lady. I would venture to say we do not have the whole story here – or even the whole Napoleon," he chuckled to himself. "Half a gallon of cloud, perhaps – a mere drop in the ocean! A puff or two around the edges! Nothing more!"

"So it's not . . . not the whole of Napoleon?" asked Mrs Mullett, fearfully.

"Oh, no, no, no!" Mr Zeus shook his head vehemently, so that his hair flew wildly around his face. "You would most certainly need a great many more buckets if the whole Napoleon were suddenly to rain upon you. Oh, dear me, yes. It would be an absolute flood!"

"But where is he then?" asked Mrs Mullett. "If he's only lost one or two of his puffs, where has he got to all this time?"

"Never fear, dear lady. I shall find him!" Mr Zeus promised, and with a swirl of his rainbow cloak, he vanished, leaving Mrs Mullett blinking after the sudden shower of colour.

Napoleon had been in his cave high up on the side of Skiddaw for what seemed a very long time. He was so unhappy that he almost wished the dreadful Carrowdale Sop would come back to swallow him up. His edges were still singed and smarting and his heart was full of misery. He felt like a permanent depression and had sunk to the floor of the cave, where he was unconsciously making everything very wet and uncomfortable for the tiny creatures who lived in its cracks and crannies.

"I don't know," one spider complained to another. "We come in here to get away from the weather, and what happens? The dratted weather comes in after us!"

And he scuttled away to try to find a dry place under the floor of the cave. But suddenly it was sunshine and snow and rainbows all at once. The spider crawled out of his crack again in sheer surprise. Mr Zeus had arrived.

Napoleon affected not to notice. He was feeling too sorry for himself to make conversation and he certainly did not want to be cheered up.

"I've come to offer you your old job back," announced Mr Zeus, perching himself on a convenient boulder.

"You mean . . . you mean General on the Cold Front?" asked Napoleon incredulously. "But why? After the Scilly Isles and that snowstorm, you said you wouldn't even employ me to make your tea or taste your wine. And you called me a . . . "

"Yes, yes, dear chap, but that's all in the past," said Mr Zeus sunnily. "I feel I have misjudged you. I have been terribly impressed, er . . . from time to time . . . er, with your initiative since you came down to Earth. I really feel it's done you the world of good. That business of rescuing that odious woman with the hat – what was her name? – from that sweet little bull, which didn't look half as dangerous as she did. Simply marvellous, my dear fellow – such initiative! And confounding the Carrowdale Sop! Brilliant! That little horror's been a thorn in my side since he graduated from Cloud School. I told his mother he had criminal tendencies. The fellow's been causing depressions wherever he goes. You brought him well and truly down to size – no more steam in him than a hot sausage!"

Napoleon began to feel warm inside. Pride was beginning to return to the empty spaces in his middle. Whatever Mr Mullett might think about it, he was a success. Mr Zeus wanted him back.

"Well?" asked Mr Zeus in his lilting voice, and as he looked at Napoleon a couple of distant comets seemed to twinkle in his eyes. "Well?" he asked again. "Are you ready to come back? Your year's trial ends with the winter and it is already the back end of t' year, as your friend Mr Mullett would put it. I understand you had a little trouble down on the farm . . . " he paused and stifled a tiny giggle in

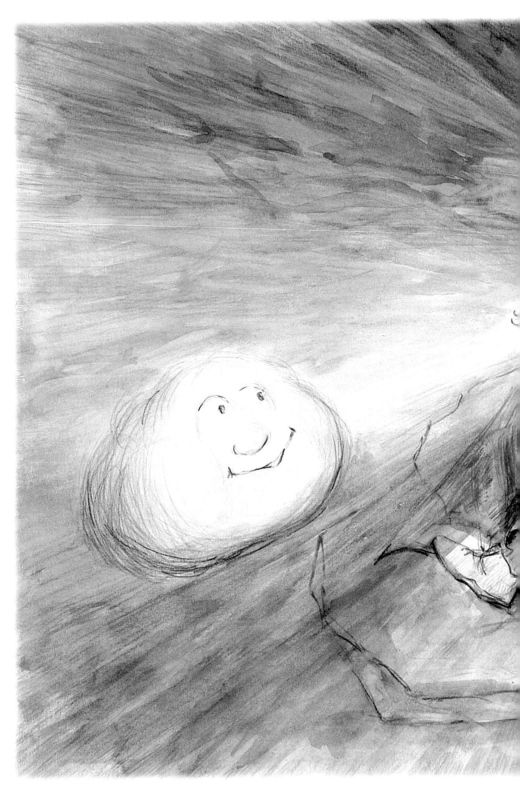

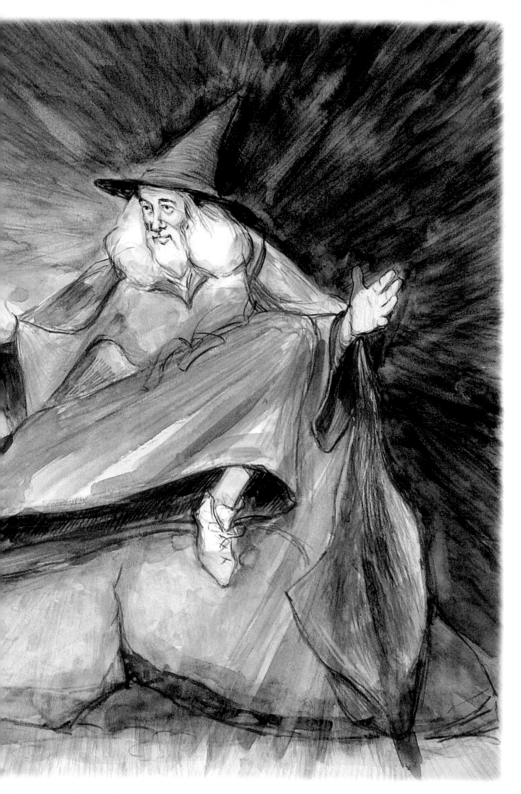

his wispy handkerchief, "Perhaps now," he continued, tucking the hanky back into his voluminous blue trousers, "would be a good time to say farewell? I'll leave you to think about it."

And suddenly where the rainbow-coloured figure had been there was nothing but a patch of sky.

General on the Cold Front! It was very tempting. But for some reason Napoleon just could not bring himself to say yes. For many days and nights he skulked in the cave at the top of the fell, making life thoroughly miserable for all those creatures who were forced to live under a permanent cloud.

Why couldn't he just take Mr Zeus up on his offer? The more he thought about Mr Mullett and how cross he was going to be, the less he could bring himself to go down and face the music. What was it Hubert the Thunderhead had told him? Mortals never forgave you if you damaged their television sets. And what about Mrs Mullett? She had been so addicted to the six o'clock news, even though it and the state of the world troubled her. Even now she was probably thinking angry thoughts about him. But if he went back to living in the sky, he could be a General again, organise the Cold Fronts, boss the anticyclones about, stir up a storm or two. All the other clouds would obey his orders and respect him.

How often had Mr Mullett taken the wind out of his puffs just by looking at him if Napoleon had been showing off just a little bit? It was certainly tempting to say yes to Mr Zeus . . .

Then one day, when the snow was walking the fells with a wide, white cloak and a bitter wind was moaning through the gullies, Napoleon, still undecided, rode out onto the icy morning for the

first time for many weeks. If I were a General again, he thought as a spiteful gust slammed him back against the rock face, I could order this nasty little wind to mind it's p's and q's. He looked upwards at the grey, flocking snow and the wildly galloping clouds. More exciting than a life with sheep! He looked down the fell, remembering bitterly the episode of the sheep dip.

But then, quite suddenly, he thought of that homely kitchen with its rocking chair and the hateful cat and Mr Mullett's cap on the nail by the door; Old Tom wuffling in his sleep after rabbits and Mrs Mullett baking bread in the coke oven. And all at once it did not matter a jot about being a General on the Cold Front and bossing the anticyclones about. He could not bear the thought of leaving the Mulletts and the farm for ever. A great wave of homesickness billowed through him like the wind from the sea and, with his edges quivering, he struggled against the snowy updraught, trying to fly down the fell to the folk and the warm hearth below.

"It'll spoil my Christmas," Mrs Mullett confided in Old Tom as she shredded cotton wool for the Christmas tree. "Just thinking of him up there somewhere in all this terrible clarty weather near breaks my heart."

And she took off her glasses and wiped them vigorously with a tuft of cotton wool. A few strands fell on Old Tom's nose and he skittered off round the kitchen, pawing violently at his muzzle and sneezing.

"Aye, I do miss him," Mrs Mullett went on as she balanced precariously on the milking stool. "Seems as though a bit of life's

gone out of t' house. Mr Mullett's feeling it too – they had some queer good cracks ovver in yon byre."

Mrs Mullett reached behind her for more cotton wool, but instead her fingers encountered something tingly and wet. She looked over her shoulder. There was cotton wool everywhere - on the table, drooping onto the floor, dancing round the lamp. And as she watched, the cotton wool floated over to the tree and covered it in imitation snow.

"Well, bless me," said Mrs Mullett. "It's our Napoleon!"

Mr Mullett was sitting with Snowball in her stable waiting for her to foal. He had not had his tea and was feeling hungry and irritable. But he dared not leave the mare, who looked as though she might produce at any minute. Where the dickens was Mrs Mullett? It was getting late. Tomorrow was Christmas Day and there was so much to be done. If only Napoleon was here, Mr Mullett thought regretfully, I could leave him in charge while I went in and had a warm. He missed Napoleon too; there was no getting away from it.

Suddenly the inside of the stable became damp with mist. The lamp went out with a psst. Mr Mullett stood up from the straw bale where he had been sitting and smacked his head on a low beam.

"I suppose its thoo, come back again to plague the living daylights oot o' me?" he asked the misty darkness.

There was a nervous giggle from somewhere above him.

"Thoo always was a dummel-head!" added Mr Mullett, not too unkindly. Napoleon stretched his puffs a little. Mr Mullett,

it seemed, was glad to see him back.

"And now," Mr Mullett said sternly, "thoo can mek thisell useful for a change and watch over Snowball, while I ga in and have a cup of tea and a bit of a warm. It's that snerpy in here, mi hands are near droppin' off. Let me know if owt happens!"

And with that he was gone. He didn't mention the television, thought Napoleon to himself with some relief.

It was good to be home. Even though Mr Mullett had forgotten to relight the lamp, the stable was a comforting place to be, with its sweet smell of straw and the occasional gentle whickering of Snowball feeling the peculiar sensations in her belly. Napoleon floated up among the high oak rafters and settled down for a snooze. When he awoke, the stable was filled with rainbow light. Mr Zeus was sitting in the straw watching a spindle-legged chestnut foal as it staggered to its feet and began to nudge its mother for milk.

"Happy Christmas!" said Mr Zeus without looking up.

Mr Mullett staggered back into the stable rubbing his eyes, having fallen asleep from sheer exhaustion in front of the kitchen fire.

"Dost tha know it's past midnight?" he asked grumpily. Then he caught sight of the foal. He stopped short. Mr Zeus, invisible to the farmer, leaned forward and guided the little creature on to the mare's udder.

"Well, if that don't beat hen racin'," said Mr Mullett. "And what wus thoo doin', I'd like to know?" he said, looking up at Napoleon. "I should ha' known better than to trust a puffed-oop puddle of steam which nivver did owt but haffle and maffle and get in t'road.

Trust thoo to stay awake? Trust thoo? There's more sense in standing in t' middle of motorway!"

Some things never changed. Napoleon was in trouble again. Mr Mullett stomped over to where the foal nuzzled milkily into his mother's flank. He ran a calloused hand along the little creature's withers.

"Fine foal!" he said gruffly. "And that canny Snowball did it all by herself. She nivver did that before. It's a miracle!"

Mr Mullett mused wonderingly, staring right through the space where Mr Zeus had been. From somewhere above the rafters came a silvery laugh.

"All by herself," repeated Mr Mullett, still shaking his head, and he went off to make up a bucket of hot mash for the mare.

"But you did it!" said Napoleon to Mr Zeus indignantly and to nowhere in particular. "You did it and he didn't even see you!"

"It was still a miracle," said a laughing voice from somewhere above him. "Believe me, some of the greatest miracles happen in stables. I saw one once," the voice echoed dreamily among the rafters, "it was the greatest miracle of all. It put us all in our place. Nothing was ever quite the same after that . . . "

The rainbow light was slipping away.

"Goodbye, Napoleon, for the moment," the voice whispered around the cobwebby windows. "Take care of the mortals. Remember, you have touched their lives with Sky Magic and they have touched yours with the Earth. Goodbye . . . "

Napoleon, strangely stirred, wafted out of the stable and away across the rutted, frozen yard towards the lights of Mrs Mullett's Christmas tree shining in the kitchen window.   THE END.

The following are definitions of Cumbrian dialect words in the order that they appear in the text of the book.

summat - *something*
neet - *night*
cushed - *quietened*
yan - *one*
aye - *yes*
reet - *right*
maest - *most*
tha knows - *you know*
thowt - *thought*
wus - *was*
in't - *in the*
nivver - *never*
wid - *with*
clood - *cloud*
gowk - *idiot*
owt - *anything*
aboot - *about*
mair - *more*
nee mair - *no more*
watter - *water*
t'wedder - *the weather*
nowt - *nothing*
garn - *going*
tek - *take*
yer - *you*
thoos - *you've*
thisell - *yourself*
missell - *myself*

fer - *for*
mekking - *making*
aw - *all*
tha's - *you are*
cem - *came*
thoo - *you*
oop - *up*
doon - *down*
deur - *do*
poddish - *porridge*
steg on a het girdle - *gander on a hot plate*
yan, tyan, tethera, methera, pimp, sethera, lethera, hovera, dovera, dick. Yan-a-dick, tyan-a-dick, tethera-a-dick, methera-a-dick, bumfit. yan-a-bumfit, tyan-a-bumfit, tethera-a-bumfit, methera-a-bumfit, giggot. *(The Cumbrian shepherd's traditional method of counting 1 - 20).*
ga - *go*
tatie - *potato*
gang ahint - *go ahead (Shepherd's command to sheepdog to set off on what is called the outrun).*

sprackling - *fine rain*
t'fwoks - *the folks*
dummel heed - *a stupid person*
steean - *stone*
git garn - *get going*
mi - *my*
noo - *now*
by Gaw - *by God*
mebbe - *maybe*
clattin' - *gossiping*
owd - *old*
clarty - *dirty*
blatherskyte - *a gossip*

lig and smit - *marks of identification on sheep*
wuk - *work*
av - *have*
doot - *doubt*
ovver - *over*
heaf - *home territory of the sheep (as in hefted sheep)*
gitten - *got*
mek - *make*
snerpy - *cold*
haffle and maffle - *make a fuss, flap about.*

ACKNOWLEDGMENTS

Special thanks are due to Keith Richardson, Editor of Cumbria Life magazine for his commitment to the book, his encouragement and advice on dialect, and to Jonathan Law, Cumbria Life designer for bringing it all together and to David Boyd for his superb and atmospheric illustrations.
Also to all the Cumbria Life team for their support.

Very many thanks are due to Di Denney, my original editor at Chatto & Windus for her unfailing support for this my very first book back in 1982 and setting me on the path as a writer.

Many thanks to Jill Jackson for advice on hill farming in Cumbria.